Strong Courage

By

Ronna M. Bacon

Joshua 1:9. Have I not commanded you? Be strong and of good courage; do not be afraid, nor be dismayed, for the Lord your God is with you wherever you go.

Table of Contents

She struggled to get free, to run from the teenager holding her arms, even as he laughed in glee at her distress. Tears of fear and hurt streaked her face as she struggled against his tight grasp, feeling the bruises forming on her wrists. How would she explain those to her mom and dad? She fell onto the damp dirt floor of the shed, her hands and knees digging in as the door slammed behind her and she heard the lock click in place. Pitch black greeted her as she opened her eyes. She jumped to her feet, running to the door and pounding on it, shoving at it to get it to open, her cries and pleas for help unanswered. It stood solid, bare traces of light coming around the edge.

Whoever had trapped her here had made sure she would be in the dark. Terror rose within her as she heard scurrying sounds in the blackness. She slid into a corner, her knees raised. She wrapped her arms around her knees, even as she tried to see something, anything at all. She gradually lost focus, drifting down into darkness within her. Terror had completely shut her down.

She didn't hear the door as it opened hours later or see as a light shone around, finding her huddled form. The man reached for her, dragging her to her feet and from the building. He gave her water, brushed off her clothes and then headed her in the direction of her home. She stumbled as she moved forward, not focused on her footsteps. She reached her home, climbed the stairs and then crawled into her bed, not seeing any of her family. She didn't see her mother stand an hour later over her before her hand reached to brush across her hair.

She woke the next morning, terror driving everything deep within her. She vaguely recalled the threats the man had made against her, against her brother, against her parents. She would let nothing happen to them. She would remain silent about what had happened.

Chapter 1

$\mathcal{H}$ands jammed into his windbreaker pocket, Silas Peters pulled up his collar and tugged his ball cap further down on his head, shoulders hunched against the damp wind. He stared at the white clapboarded church he pastored from where he stood in the parking lot, puddles from the torrential downpours that happened over the last ten days surrounding him. He watched the activity as the disaster crew the church had hired set up to go in and assess the damage and then set up their pumps to drain off the water that had flooded the basement. He sighed. Today was Friday and it looked as if he's have to find another place for the congregation of Elmton Community Church to meet on Sunday. They certainly wouldn't be meeting here.

He turned as he heard his name called and saw the one of the church board, Ray Walker, making his way towards him, reaching out a hand to shake his.

"What's the situation, Silas?"

Silas shook his head. "They haven't gone in yet, but I snuck a peek through the windows. It's up to the third or fourth stair down. It's bad."

Ray sighed. "That's what I thought, given the rain we've had. I don't think I've ever seen rain like this, not this bad. Any plans for Sunday?"

Silas shrugged. "So far, no. Any building that would be big enough is taken up with evacuees. And I don't think we can do an outdoor service, given the forecast. And we can't not do a service. Our people need it, need to come together."

"That they do. Is the internet still up?" Ray was running possible solutions through his mind.

"So far we have power and internet. Why?"

"Can we do a live broadcast, get our people together in various homes and connect that way, that is if we can't come up with a solution of a building?"

Silas thoughtfully nodded. "It would work. It wouldn't be ideal for what we want, but it's a possible solution. Andrew McBeth was working on a solution for me and is to let me know. Jonah's offered his sales barn -

he's working on clearing it out and bringing in chairs. I think that might be the solution."

Ray grinned as he nodded. "I like that one. Bless Jonah. I say let him know that's what we'll do. What about parking?"

"Car pooling. We can meet here and use the van to shuttle. Jonah also said he has a friend with a bus that we could use."

"Sounds like you have it under control." He nodded towards where they could see a police officer and one of the disaster response crew heading into the building. "Now, we just need to pray there's not a lot of damage there."

"That we do." Silas jammed his hands back into his pockets, shivering against the chill wind even as the sun started to break through the clouds.

Madigan Browne sometimes hated her job on a disaster restoration crew. This was one of those times. She hated that the church she attended when she could had been flooded. She turned to the young officer with her.

"Sam, let me go down first. I don't think we'll get far, not from what I'm hearing." She stepped down the three steps she could and then one more into the water.

She gripped the handrail with her one hand and looked around.

"Do you have the flashlight?" She grasped it as he handed it to her and flashed it around, searching the area. "So far, I think we should be able to run the hoses and start the pumps." She turned to the officer crouched down the step behind her. "Do you see anything out of the ordinary?"

"No, not that I can see."

Madian flashed the light once more, bringing its beam back to something she had caught a glimpse of. Her face blanching, she reached for Sam's arm. "Over there. Is that what I think it is?"

Sam ducked lower, his eyes following the light and he groaned. "You're right. We're out of here, Madigan. Now. It's a crime scene. We'll need to bring in people. I never expected to find a body here."

"This has never ever happened to me. Never!" She turned, Sam's hand gripping her arm as she slipped and then she followed him up the stairs and out the door. "Why, Lord? This was supposed to be a simple job. Now look at the mess we're in. Did we really have to find a body?"

Sam smiled as she grumbled out a prayer. He was friends with Madigan and her brother Mitchell and knew how Madigan prayed.

"Over here, Madigan. I'll call it in. I don't think you'll be going anywhere for a while."

She stood by the M&M Disaster Response van and nodded, pulling off her heavy rubber boots and then her overalls.

"I know. Now it's just a hurry up and wait situation, isn't it?" She sat on the bumper to pull on her runners and tie them.

He nodded. "Someone will have to take your statement as well as mine." He handed her a bottle of water before he turned away.

Silas watched as the two had exited the building and stood talking before Sam walked over to his patrol vehicle and pulled open the door, reaching in for his radio. He frowned as he watched the other person pulling off boots and overalls, then slumping down on the bumper, arms crossed. He walked over, his head tilted as he recognized Madigan.

"Madigan?"

Her head shot up as he spoke. "Silas? I should have expected you to be here."

"Where else would I be?" He was genuinely puzzled by her answer.

"I'm sorry. It's not a good day and getting worse every moment." She stared at the church, a frown on her face, before she pulled the pony tail holder and shook out her auburn hair.

"What's wrong?" Silas moved to sit beside her, ready to be a pastor if she needed one.

She pointed with the water bottle she held. "That's the problem."

"How bad is the flood?" Silas turned to stare at the church.

"It's up to the fourth step. That's not the issue. We have a body in the water."

Silas spun back to stare at her, fast enough he had to grab the side of the bumper to stay seated. "A body? In the basement? Who? How?"

"Yes, a body in the basement." Sam spoke from beside him. "Not another word, Madigan, until you give your statement."

She nodded, even as she took a drink from the bottle. "I know, Sam. Just get this over with so I can do my job."

Sam shook his head and then asked Silas to come with him. "I need you to stay away from her until she gives her statement."

Silas nodded, his hand rubbing down his cheek. "Sure. I'm sorry. I didn't know."

"No, you wouldn't have, not unless you're responsible." He held up his hands as Silas stared at him. "I'm just saying that. I know you're not responsible. Here's Andrew and the crew. We'll get her statement. Then can you sit with her for a while? She's really shaken."

"I know. She's not used to this."

"No, she's not." Sam eyed his pastor. "You aren't either. You're shaken."

Silas nodded. "That I am. This is not what we expected, is it?" He sighed as he turned away, heading for the picnic table sitting near the parking lot and pulling out his phone. He had to call Ray Walker or Art Wayne, let them know what had just happened. He knew Andrew would find him soon.

He looked up about an hour later as a hot cup of coffee was set in front of him.

Madigan slid onto the seat across from him, a look of sympathy on her face.

"Silas? You okay?"

He shook his head. "I should be asking you that, Madigan. Are you okay?"

She shrugged. "What can I say? I've gone into places most people wouldn't even think about going into. Places where bodies have been. I've just never found one myself." She sipped her own cup of coffee. "Drink. You need to get warmed up."

He nodded, even he pulled the top from the cup. "I won't ask you anything about it. I'm sure I'll be suspected."

She nodded. "Likely, but you're clear. You wouldn't have done something like this." Her eyes followed the movements across the parking lot. "They'll be a while. There's not much evidence, though, and I'll likely be able to start the pumps this afternoon or evening. Michell will take over tonight for me." She laid her head down on her folded arms. She was exhausted, had been before this started, and now this.

"Madigan? Anything I can do?"

She shook her head, blinking back tears at the sympathy she heard. "Nothing.

There's nothing anyone can do.   Thanks anyway."

Silas watched her, before he heard their names called and turned.   Andrew was beckoning for them to come towards him. They rose, walking that way, silence between them, when the roaring of an engine caught their ears. Silas turned, giving a shout as he wrapped Madigan in an arm and pulled her with him as he threw himself away from the truck rushing towards them. He felt the thud of the truck on his body even as he flew through the air, landing hard, Madigan still wrapped tight in his arms. His head hit with a thud and he didn't hear the shouts of the onlookers, didn't see Andrew running towards him, the patrol officers taking off, siren and lights on, after the truck.   He slumped into unconsciousness, his only prayer that in some way, he had protected Madigan from harm.

Chapter 2

*A*ndrew dropped to his knees in the mud puddle, his hands reaching out to Silas, feeling for a pulse, then feeling along his body for any injury. He heard the calls for paramedics and felt a hand on his shoulder. He looked up. Mitchell Browne stood there, his face white, his eyes on his sister.

"Andrew?" Mitchell moved to the other side of the couple on the ground, his shaky hand reaching out to touch his sister. "What happened? I just got here and was walking towards you."

"Someone ran them down." He looked up. "Madigan found a body in the basement."

"A body!" Mitchell sat back on his heels. "A body? In the church?"

Andrew nodded as he stood aside for the paramedics. "A body. We've just started the investigation. It would be late this evening before it's cleared for you to start the pumps."

Mitchell nodded as he watched his sister being worked on, her voice pain filled but quiet as she answered the questions she was asked. He turned so he could see the church, watching the activity there. He sighed, knowing he needed to call his parents, reaching for his phone.

Andrew watched as the paramedics maneuvered Silas onto a backboard and then onto a stretcher, his neck protected with a collar. He was still unconscious, blood dripping down his face from a cut on his forehead, his clothing soaked from the water he had landed in. Andrew was frustrated. He had received word that the truck had disappeared, his men not able to find it. He watched as the two were loaded into ambulances before the ambulances crept through the lot and then hit the street, lights and sirens on. Mitchell waved at him as he headed for his truck.

Andrew turned, studying the line of flight of the truck. He had no idea who would have done this. As far as he knew, Silas didn't have any enemies and he didn't think Madigan did either. He had work to do here before he could head to the hospital. He shook his head as he headed for the scene near the church.

❁ ❁ ❁ ❁

Madigan shifted on the hospital bed, her body aching. She was lucky, she knew. Nothing broken. No cuts, just bruises. Silas had protected her from that. Her eyes watched her brother pacing. Her parents were on their way but hadn't got there yet.

"Mitchell? How's Silas?"

Mitchell stopped and then came to stand beside her. "God was looking after you today, Madigan. It could have been so much worse."

"I know. But you didn't answer my question. How's Silas?"

"I haven't heard, not since they loaded him up to come in. He was unconscious. They weren't sure how bad he was." He stared at his sister, searching her face for something. "What happened?"

She shrugged, regretting the movement. "I don't know. You know what I found, don't you? Silas and I were sitting at the picnic table, Andrew called for us, and we were just walking across the parking lot. Minding our own business. Walking across the church parking lot when some lunatic ran us down." She saw the grin he quickly suppressed. "You can laugh. It wasn't you that was run down. It was me!"

"And Silas. What about the body?"

She sighed. "I'm not supposed to talk about it, you know, but I have to tell Mom and Dad because it affects the business. I won't forget seeing that body, Mitchell. I have no idea if it was a man or a woman. Sam made me leave as soon as we saw it."

"I haven't heard anything else." He hooked a foot around a chair and dragged it over, sitting down.

She shivered, not from cold but from what she had felt as she saw the body. "I don't think it was an accident, Mitchell. They would have had to break into the church, unless they had a key." She laid her head back. "Please tell me they don't suspect our pastor."

"I have no idea." Mitchell's head turned as he looked over his shoulder. "Here's Andrew. You can ask him that."

Andrew stood for a moment, clearing his thoughts, his eyes on Madigan. God was good, he thought, protecting both of them.

"Andrew? How's Silas?" Madigan's quiet voice broke into this thoughts.

"Very lucky, Madigan. Nothing broken. He's still out, but they said that's to be expected from the blow he took to the head."

"Unconscious? Andrew!" Madigan hands covered her mouth.

He nodded. "His head hit pretty hard when he went down. He did what he could to protect you, Madigan, taking the brunt of the hit and the fall." His eyes watched her as she absorbed what he was saying.

She finally nodded. "Who's with him?"

"Phoebe came in and is sitting with him right now. Ray's working to have someone with him all the time." Andrew sighed. "This hasn't been a good day for you, has it?"

"No, it hasn't. I've certainly had better days." Mitchell and Andrew laughed at her disgruntled tone. "It's not funny." She shifted on the bed, pain causing her to frown. "What do you know about the body in the church, Andrew?"

"Not a lot. It was a male, early thirties, the coroner said. He'll know more once he's completed his examination." He held up a hand. "No, I won't say anything more for now. I just stopped by to see how you were doing. We'll likely have more questions for you over the next few days. Just routine." He exchanged a glance with Mitchell before he walked away

Mitchell finally rose, pacing the room. Madigan took a look at him and finally spoke.

"Go, find out what you want to know. I can see that you're not comfortable here. You'll need to head back to the church."

He turned, nodding. "Mom and Dad should be here soon. Will you be okay if I leave?"

She stared at him. "Of course, I will. I'm in a hospital, lots of people around me, nurses coming in every few minutes. Why wouldn't I be?"

Mitchell stared at her. He loved his sister deeply, but grew frustrated sometimes at the way she just flippantly took things that happened. "I'll be back later. I need to see if I can get the pumps up and running." He dropped a kiss on her cheek before walking away.

Madigan stared at him, before laying her head back. She was suddenly fatigued, more than she could ever remember being, and her eyes slid closed as she slept. She didn't see the older man who stood in her doorway before walking over to her bed, to stand watching her before he turned and walked away. He shook his head. The fool, he thought, he went after him when he shouldn't have. There were too many people around. It was only a matter of time before they found him and linked him to himself.

The man made his way through the floor until he found Silas' room and stopped at the doorway, his head turning as he searched for the nurses. He couldn't get near him right now, he saw, and walked away before anyone recognized him. That, he didn't want. He needed to stay unknown, at least for now.

His head turning restlessly on his pillow, Silas groaned with the pain. He couldn't remember what happened. He blinked, taking in the low lighting and then the IV in his arm. He looked around, frowning, pain shooting through his head. He didn't remember where he was. Who was he? He couldn't remember his name. He reached for the call button, pushing it even as he lay back, exhausted.

The nurse appeared in his vision, a smile on her face. "You're awake, Silas. How are you feeling?"

He stared at her, not sure if she was calling him by the right name. "My name's Silas?"

She turned from where she had removed the IV line, patting a bandage into place. "Sure. You're Silas Peters, pastor of Elmton Community Church. You don't remember?"

He shook his head, regretting it at the pain shooting through it. He tried to fight through the pain, but it was a losing battle and he slid back into darkness, leaving the nurse staring at him before she headed for the desk and the phone. Middle of the night or not, she needed to talk with his treating physician. He would want to know that Silas couldn't even remember his name.

Andrew stood at Silas' bedside the next morning, watching as Silas roused. The nurse had given him the news, and he prayed that Silas would remember this morning. His people needed him at this time. Andrew and his team had not found out who had run Silas down, nor had they determined the identity of the body in the church. He needed to talk to Silas but it didn't look like it would happen today.

He turned as he heard footsteps behind him and greeted the physician from the church.

"John. How is he?"

"That's a good question, Andrew. I'm told he was awake during the night but couldn't remember who he was."

Andrew stared at him and then at Silas. "Are you serious? Silas?"

John Knox nodded. "Silas. Let's see how he is this morning. With both of us here from the church, it should be interesting." He pulled his stethoscope from around his neck and listened to Silas' heart and lungs, before stepping back and studying him. "He should be okay. It's the knock on the head I'm worried about."

Andrew nodded. "I would guess that." He watched as Silas' eyes blinked open and he frowned.

"Silas? Can you hear me?"

Silas turned his head towards the voice, a frown on his face. "Who's Silas?"

Andrew and John shared a look. "You are." John stood, watching Silas' face.

"No, I don't think I am. Who am I?" Silas groaned as he moved.

"You're Silas Peters and you're the pastor at our church." Andrew moved into Silas' line of sight.

"I am?" Silas laid his head back, his eyes closing. "I have such a headache. What did I do?"

"You were run down by a truck yesterday and hit your head on the pavement in the church parking lot. You really don't remember?"

Silas' eyes popped open and he stared at Andrew. "Run down? Why?"

"That we don't know yet. We're working on it." He realized Silas had no idea who he was or that they were good friends. "I'm Andrew McBeth, Chief of Police. This is Dr. John Knox. He's one of our deacons at church."

Silas sighed. "Forgive me. I just don't remember." His breathing evened out as he slept again.

"He'll sleep for a while. His scans were clear last night. I don't think we need to repeat them, unless he continues as he is." John stood for a moment, then pointed at the door. "We'll let him sleep. Call me later and see what the status is."

Andrew took one last look at Silas, his heart raising a prayer for his complete healing. "I'll do that, John. Thank you."

He moved towards Madigan's room, finding it empty. He turned to see Mitchell watching him.

"She's checked out, has she?" Mitchell shook his head. "She was supposed to wait for me."

"She's gone? Where can I find her?" Andrew turned to walk with Mitchell towards the elevators.

"Knowing Madigan, likely at work. She won't go home, not when we have so much to do. Don't worry, Mom won't let her out on the road. She'll keep her in the office."

"Then, I'll head there at some point. Thanks, Mitchell." Andrew walked back to his car, his thoughts mixed. Who was the body and why the church? Was Silas a target or was it just something random?

Chapter 3

*M*adigan snuck a peek behind her as she stood in the doorway of the hospital room, then walked quietly over to where Silas lay. Mitchell had tracked her down, told her off, and then informed her that her rescuer couldn't remember who he was. She didn't believe him. That's why she was sneaking up on Silas in his hospital bed.

She stood, a frown on her face, as she studied the face of her pastor, noting how young he looked, taking in the dark brown hair, knowing his closed eyelids hid his dark brown eyes.

She prayed as she stood, prayed for healing, for Andrew to find out who had done this. She raised her head, startled to see Silas' eyes on her.

"Hi."

He wet his lips and then spoke. "Hi, yourself. I'm sorry. I don't remember your name."

She shook her head. "I'm Madigan. I'm the one you saved the other day."

"Saved? How?" He was puzzled and his face showed it.

"They didn't tell you what happened?" When he shook his head and then grimaced with the pain, she sighed. "I thought they had. You took the brunt of the truck hitting us and the fall, saving me from injury. It was in the church parking lot." She searched his face, seeing a slight spark of remembrance.

"I see myself falling. I didn't know why. I really saved you?" He rubbed his face with his hands. He shifted in the bed, his hand going down to his leg, pressing against the pain there. "I'm sorry. I'm don't remember."

"I know you don't but I wish you did." She pulled up a chair and sat, her eyes on him. "You can't remember anything at all?"

He shook his head. "Not really. I have flashes of stuff that I don't understand." He watched her face, her amber eyes, a frown on his face. How close was he to her, anyway, he wondered. She looks like someone he would like to know better.

She sighed. "Then, I guess the best thing to do is to walk you through your home.

We can't do the church. Besides the basement being still flooded, it's a crime scene."

"Crime scene?" Silas choked on his words. "A crime scene?"

She nodded. "You really don't remember, do you? I went down to see about laying in the hoses to drain the basement and found a body in the water."

He shook his head. "I don't remember that at all. You're sure?" When she nodded, he sighed. "Guess I need to get out of here and see what I can do." He peered at her. "Why would you be there laying hoses?"

"I work for my parents with their disaster response company. That's what I was doing there, getting ready to lay hoses to drain the basement." She watched for a reaction, seeing none.

"I don't remember that at all." He stared at the ceiling, frustration evident.

"When are they letting you out?"

"The doctor said today, but I have to have someone with me. He tells me I live on my own." He looked over at her to verify that.

"You do. That's why Mom wants you to come to their place." She looked around as a nurse entered and then rose. "I'll be outside when you're ready to go."

Silas watched her walk away, a slight frown on his face. Now, why was she doing this, he wondered? He looked up at the ceiling, needing to pray but not knowing how to frame his words. It was like a part of him was missing.

The nurse fussed around him, finally leaving him alone, his clothes on the bed beside him. Frustrated at how hard it was to get dressed, he eventually pushed the call button for the nurse. She appeared, pushing a wheel chair. Silas frowned at that, then sat in it, knowing he didn't have the strength to walk very far.

Madigan watched carefully as she helped Silas walk the few steps into their home and to the living room, where he sank down onto the couch with a nod of thanks, short of breath and unable to frame any words. She headed for the kitchen, where she found her mother.

"How is he, dear?" Mary Browne turned to speak with her daughter, stopping as she caught a look on Madigan's face and then smiled.

"Tired beyond belief. Sore. He shouldn't have been released yet." She looked at her mother, tears just beneath the surface. "I can't handle it, Mom, that he's like this because of me."

Mary hugged her daughter, then stood back. "God is in control, Mads. Now, take him a cup of proper coffee and some toast. I'm sure he's ready for something better than hospital food."

Madigan laughed at that, picking up the tray and heading for the living room, stopping short as she saw Silas stretched out on the couch, sound asleep. She set the tray down quietly and reached for the blanket her mother kept on the back of the couch, tucking it gently around Silas, her hand brushing the hair back from his forehead in an automatic gesture. She turned and headed back to the kitchen and conversation and prayer with her mother.

Late that afternoon, Silas finally roused, his head feeling clearer. He sat up, waiting for the dizziness that never came. He searched the room, a frown in place. He didn't recognize it, not really, but he knew it wasn't his place. Where was he? He scrubbed his hands down his face, feeling the whiskers and knowing he needed to shave. He stood, unsteady for a moment, then followed the sound of voices to the kitchen.

Mary looked over from the stove and smiled.

"Silas. Good to see you on your feet. Do you want something to eat or just some coffee for now?" She held up a wooden spoon. "I've soup if you want it."

Silas frowned, then spoke. "If I could clean up first, then coffee, I would appreciate it."

Mary nodded, then pointed behind him. "Come. We've got you set up down the hall in the guest suite. It has its own bath and Mitchell stopped by your place and grabbed you some clothes. I hope that was all right."

Silas shrugged. "He probably knows better than I do where I live."

"How's the headache?"

"Still there but much better. Thank you." He looked around. "Your family's not here?"

"Matthew and Mitchell are still at work. Madigan is in the home office, finishing off some reports. She'll be done in about half an hour." She didn't let him see the small smile on her face.

Silas stared down at the pile of clothes, not recognizing them. He reached and felt the jeans and dark T-shirt, realizing that they were his but he had no recollection of them. Lord, he prayed, they tell me I'm a pastor. Guess that means we're on good speaking terms. I have no idea why You let this happen, but You have. Heal me. Guide me as I walk this path. I know I can't do it alone. Don't let me hurt anyone. He turned to stare at the door, knowing Madigan was in the house, and wanting to find her. She was his connection to what had happened and who he was.

Madigan looked up as he appeared in the doorway of the office. He had followed her voice, desperate to see her, to know that she was still there. She smiled, her smile lighting up her face.

"Silas? Are you feeling better? Come. Sit here." She pulled a chair forward for him and watched as he sank down into it with a breath of relief.

"Thank you, Madi. I appreciate that." He watched her, wanting to question her but not sure if he should.

"Here. Mom brought in some coffee for us. And some toast for you. She said you couldn't wait for supper for something to eat." She placed the tray on the table beside him. "Now, eat. I don't want to get into trouble with Mom because you didn't."

He gave a small laugh and reached for the coffee, inhaling the scent of it. "Your mother grinds her own beans?"

"She does. Not many people pick up on that." She sat back in a matching chair, folding her legs under her. "Eat. Then we talk. I can see you have questions." She laughed at the look on his face.

Finally, he set the tea plate down and looked at her. "Tell me, Madi. What can you tell me?"

She tilted her head to watch his face. He was the first one to shorten her name to that, and she kind of liked that. Her family always called her Mads. "I'm not sure how much I can tell you. You've been pastor here since you graduated from seminary, about nine, ten years, something like that. You live in a house near the church. Your parents are serving overseas with a mission and we haven't been able to reach them yet. Communication is poor and spotty at best where they are. You have no siblings." She grinned at him. "What else would you like to know?"

He laughed, then frowned. "That tells me some things. Will you walk me through my house?"

She stared at him. "I've never been to your home, so I'm not sure if I'm the best one to do that."

"Please, Madi? I would appreciate if you would." Silas felt like he was pleading.

Madigan looked up, seeing her father standing there, nodding. She sighed to herself. "Why not? How about tomorrow morning? That will give you a chance to get a good night's sleep. You never sleep well in the hospital, too many interruptions."

He laughed again, then stood, reaching for her hand to help her stand. She tugged at his grasp when she stood, but he didn't release her hand, not even seeming to realize he still held it. Matthew shook his head at the two, a smile on his face that Madigan frowned at.

Chapter 4

Silas stood in the living room of his home, staring around. He didn't recognize anything, taking in trust what Madigan had told him. She had followed him in and stood just behind him, watching him turn and search the room, knowing he was looking for something to stir his memory. He reached for her hand, grasping it tightly as he pulled her with him, walking through the rooms, ending up in his office.

He stood, his eyes flickering over the diplomas and certificates on the wall, the shelves loaded with books, his desk with paperwork still on it, waiting for him to come back. He walked over to the desk, finally letting go of Madigan's hand, to sink into his chair, staring at the desktop.

"What was I working on, I wonder?"

"Likely your Sunday sermon. No one blames you, Silas. You couldn't help what happened."

Silas shook his head. "Somehow, I feel like I could. I just can't shake that feeling."

She nodded as she perched on the edge of his desk, moving the paperwork over so she wouldn't disturb it. "Why do you feel like that?"

He shrugged. "I have no idea." His eyes caught her, a look in his that she couldn't place. "Help me figure out, will you, please?"

"Don't forget, the doctors said your memory will come back."

"I know. I just want it back now."

She laughed. "Impatient, are we?" She looked around the office. "Where would we start?"

"Take me to the church." He stood and reached for her hand, watching as she hesitated before giving him hers.

Silas stood in the parking lot, before turning in a circle. "Where were we?"

Madigan pointed. "We had been sitting at the picnic table and Andrew called us to come over where he was. We were about here when the truck raced through from the back entrance and nailed us. I didn't see much, other than you grabbing me and trying to jump for safety."

"You weren't hurt?" He turned, his eyes assessing her.

"Just bumps and bruises." She shrugged. "You protected me and took the fall, as they say."

He nodded, walking towards the church. "You said there was a body in the basement?"

"There was. Mitchell's been here, pumping out the water."

"Can we go in?"

She shook her head. "Not yet. It hasn't been cleared yet by the police."

He frowned. He had placed his hope on going through the church. "Well, that's that then. Now what?"

"Now what, we can tour the town, see if anything rings a bell with you."

He laughed, his walk steadier as they made their way to her car. "Let's do that. Anything else you can suggest?"

She shrugged, then turned in a circle, her eyes searching. Someone was watching them, she could feel the evil there. But who and why?

Silas looked past her, a shuttered look on his face as he watched the man approach them. "Do you know this man, Madi?"

She looked around him. "No, I don't. He looks as if he really wants something."

Silas shoved her behind him as the man approached them, anger radiating from him. "Peters."

"I'm sorry. Do I know you?"

"You should. You're the one who destroyed my family years ago. I've been trying to find you. You'll pay for that." The man shook in his rage, barely able to get his words out.

Silas shook his head. "I'm sorry, once again. I have no idea what you're talking about."

"Liar. Of course you do." Before Silas could react, the man's fist connected with his jaw, sending him flying to the ground, Madigan standing in shock before she dropped down beside him, her hands reaching for him.

The man stood for a moment, then grabbing her arm, pulled her up and with him. She struggled to free her arm, finally twisting it free and running from him. He chased her, his body launched at her to take her down to the ground. She struggled to get away, finally scratching at his face and eyes until he cursed and reached for his face. She wriggled from beneath him and ran, stumbling until she regained her feet. She hid in the woods, trying to catch her breath, her head back against a tree, her eyes sliding closed. She could hear the angry stomping footsteps near her before they faded. She finally peeked around the tree, seeing him gone.

Her phone in her hand, she ran back to where Silas lay, dropping to her knees as she gave the information to the emergency dispatcher. She set her phone down and reached to roll Silas to his back.

His eyes flickered open and closed before he finally focused on her, his hand reaching up to touch her face.

"Madi? Are you all right?"

She nodded, as she willed back the tears she wanted to shed. "What about you? He hit you pretty good."

"Help me up. Now, it's all right. Help me sit up." He leaned back on his hands, his head hanging down as he regained his balance before he took the hand she offered and rose to his feet. "Are you sure you're okay? What did he do to you?"

"He tried to take me with him. I got away." She deliberately downplayed what had happened.

"Tell me everything. You're dirty. Did he hurt you?"

She shook her head. "He knocked me down and tried to take me with him." She repeated herself. "I got away and hid until he left." She looked up with relief as sirens sounded. "We need to get you looked at."

He nodded. "I'm all right, Madi. I'm just worried about you." His finger traced the scratches on her face. "I have no idea who that was. Do you?"

She turned as she heard car doors slamming and saw the paramedics heading their way as well as a patrol officer. "No. I don't. But he seemed to recognize you. I think he was waiting for you to come back here." She turned back to face him, her eyes searching his.

The paramedics cleared them both. The patrol officer listened to their statement, then reached for gloves, snapped them on and inspected Madigan's hands.

"We have some tissue here, Miss Browne. I'll need a team to come out and get a sample from here. Don't touch your fingers, please."

She looked down at them. "I already have, and so has Silas. I didn't know."

He shook his head as he walked back to his patrol vehicle. Silas caught her by the arm and led her over to the picnic table to sit.

She watched him, seeing something different about him. "Silas? Do you remember?"

He nodded. "I'm beginning to. Some things. I don't remember the last couple of days but I do before. It must have been the blow I took." He looked over at her, mischief sparking in his eyes. "What I don't remember is if we were a couple or not."

She gaped at him, finding realizing he was teasing. Her mouth opened, then she snapped it closed. Finally, she could speak. "Why would you say that?"

"Because I would like to think we could be. I would really like to get to know you better. Is there someone in your life?"

She shook her head. "No one." She reached to tuck her hair behind her ear but his hand on her wrist stopped her. "I forgot. I'm not to do that, am I?"

He shook his head. "No, I don't think you should." He waited for a response. "So, will you go out for dinner with me?"

She stared at him, her thoughts tumbling over one another. "Are you sure?" At his nod, she sighed. "I guess so. I'm just not sure I'm up to all that scrutiny."

"Scrutiny?" His brow wrinkled at that.

"Yeah. All that scrutiny. You never date. Now, you're asking me out."

Andrew stood for a moment watching the two, before shaking his head, muttering to himself about friends and adventures. He walked over to them, startling them when he appeared.

"Andrew? You're here? I didn't expect to see you." Silas reached to shake his hand.

"I can see you didn't." He smirked at the look on their faces. "Do you have anything to add to the statements you gave?"

"He knew me, Andrew, but I don't know how. I don't remember seeing him before. And how would I have ruined his life?" Silas missed the startled look on Andrew's face and his quick glance at Madigan, who nodded.

"Silas." Andrew waited, then spoke again. "Silas. Can you look at me for a moment?"

Silas brought his thoughts back and looked up at Andrew. "What is it?"

"When did you get your memory back?"

"My memory? Why, did I lose it?" Silas stared between the two as they stared at him, dumbfounded at his response.

"You did. Up to a while ago, you couldn't remember who you were or what you do. Nothing." Andrew's hand ran through his hair. "Now you can."

Silas shrugged, his eyes on Madigan. "Is what he's saying true?"

"It is. Before you were hit and knocked down, you didn't remember anything. Now you tell me you can remember everything except for the last few days."

Andrew was frustrated and it showed, disturbing Silas.

"I'm sorry, Andrew. I can't explain it. It just happened."

Madigan took pity on him. "The amnesia is pretty much gone, I'd say. You may not remember what exactly happened the other day."

Andrew shook his head. "You mean, all I had to do was slug you in the jaw and you'd remember?"

Silas grinned. "And that you would never do." He sobered. "I have no idea who he is, Andrew, but he was pretty desperate to try and take Madi with him."

Andrew looked sharply at him at the short-form name he used for Madigan, then at her, finding her eyes on Silas. Just great, Lord. Another couple falling in love right in front of me and in times of danger as well. Guess I can't say much, not after Phoebe and myself. "Did you give a description of him to the officer?" When they both nodded, he continued. "Okay, we'll run it and see what we can come up. Anything else you'd care to share?"

They shook their heads, both looking at him with guilty looks sliding quickly across their faces. He pocketed his notebook and pen and then stood, hands on his hips, his eyes on the church. "We've released the church, Silas. So if you want to wander through you can. The basement needs a lot of clean up, but I understand your Dad's looking after that, Madigan."

"He is. He'll have a crew in tomorrow, now that you've released the building." She reached for Silas' hand, pulling him to his feet. "Come on, let's go see what we can do about the last few days."

Andrew stood, watching them walk away hand in hand, his thoughts distant before he shook his head. That was a couple he hadn't seen coming, not at all. I guess You know what you're doing, Lord. I sure hope so, because I sure don't see them as a couple.

Chapter 5

*M*adigan looked around Silas' office, dumbfounded to find it in shambles. She turned to see him standing, hands on his head, searching the room, almost as if he would see who had tossed it.

"I'm guessing you didn't leave it like this?" She grinned as he glared at her. "No, eh?"

"Absolutely not. I never would. Is Andrew still here?"

She peeked out the window. "He is. Let me go get him." She ran from the room and he watched through the window as she flagged down his friend.

Andrew followed her through the church to the offices, seeing the damage in the secretary's room before stopping in the doorway to Silas' office. "Silas?"

"I didn't do this, Andrew, and I have no idea what they wanted. I don't keep anything real personal here, and anything to do with the congregation is always locked up tight.

The filing cabinets are knocked over, but not opened."

"I see that." Andrew walked through the room. "I'll have the crime scene team come through. Neither one of you touched anything?"

"No." Silas shook his head. "Just the door when I pushed it open. The lock was broken on it. I didn't see any sign that anyone had broken into the building."

"Mitchell would have locked up the building when his team was done yesterday." Madigan stepped back to look into the secretary's office. "I don't think they were looking for anything to steal. Computers, office equipment, video equipment still seems to be here."

Silas nodded. "I need to call Ray and let him know what's happened, and then find a locksmith."

Madigan paced across the front of the sanctuary. She had tried to leave but Silas had asked that she stay. She sensed that he needed her support and had agreed. Lord, I have no idea what's going on right now, but I know You do. Thank you for healing Silas' memory. But I have no idea what else You're doing. What is this with Silas? He's never looked at me before. No one ever has looked at me like he has.

Silas stood and watched as Madigan paced and prayed, he could tell. He looked up, seeking direction and confirmation for his feelings. He had noticed her at church whenever she was around, but her work sometimes took her away for days at a time. Lord, what's with this? Is this from You?

She turned, stopping in her tracks as she saw him standing there, a question in her eyes. He approached her, his hand coming up to cup her cheek, before he took her hand and drew her with him back to the office.

"The team's done. Andrew says we're free to tackle the office, if we want." Silas laughed at her look.

"Can we get it done in a couple of hours? Mom will have dinner ready for us soon." She glanced down at her watch.

"We can get a lot done by then. I don't think it's as bad as we thought. Andrew and the team helped me set the cabinets upright again. I'll check the contents later."

She stared around, then dropped to her knees to reach for the paperwork scattered around. "Any particular way you want to do this?"

He sighed, thinking it was going to be a bigger task than he thought, before watching Madigan quickly sort through the papers in front of her, tapping each pile neatly together. "You must have done this before."

She looked up, laughing at him. "It's not hard to sort things. You just need a system and a plan. I can tell by your paperwork that you're well organized. It looks as if they just tossed each file on top of one another." She stood, picking up an armful. "Where do you want these?"

He took them from her, lips parted to speak, when she turned and headed for another pile. He shook his head. Madi was on a mission, he thought, and I won't stand in her way. He turned with his paperwork in his hand, stilling as he looked at the top sheet. It wasn't his. Now, where had it come from? He slipped it off the pile and folded it, sticking it into his pocket. He would look at it later.

Two hours later, Madigan stood back, her eyes happy, dusting off her hands. "There, we did it, Silas. Just about back to normal."

"Thank you, Madi. Without you, I'd still be struggling with the first few pieces."

She turned with a laugh, her eyes landing on Ray as he walked into the office. "Ray? You're here." She was surprised to see him as she knew Silas hadn't called him yet.

"I am. I can see I'm too late to help, other than with the door." He help up his toolkit. "I understand you need a locksmith."

Silas started to laugh. "I forgot for a moment that's what you do. We can certainly use one. Right now, Anna and I are the only ones with keys to this office. I'd like to keep it that way, if I can."

"Not a problem." He set to work.

Madigan eyed him, a frown on her face, thoughts running through her mind. She hadn't heard Silas call for a locksmith and she knew Andrew hadn't. She would need to ask Silas later if he had.

As they walked back to her car, she sighed, knowing she needed to broach the subject.

"Silas, did you call Ray to come?"

He stopped, pulling her to a stop with him. "Come to think of it, no. I hadn't had a chance to call anyone. Why?"

"Then how did he know when to show up? Andrew wouldn't have called, leaving it to you. You didn't call. I didn't call. So how did he come to be there?"

Silas stared at her, his thoughts catching what she was meaning. "I see. That's a problem, now, isn't it? I'll have to think that one through."

She nodded as she headed away from the church. "You're still coming for dinner, aren't you, or do I have to take to your place?"

"Dinner, I think, Madi. We still need to talk about the dinner I want to take you to."

She glanced over at him as he stared out the side window. "It's not necessary, Silas."

He turned, catching her glance before she looked forward again. "It is, Madi. It is very necessary and very important for me to do that."

She was silent, not knowing how to respond.

Chapter 6

Silas paced his home office, his thoughts on his church office. What had they been looking for, he pondered? He didn't keep anything important to him there. It was all church information. He had emailed all the board members, letting them know what had transpired and that nothing related to church business or the congregation had been exposed. He still felt threatened by the break-in.

He turned back to his desk, pulling out a metal box, and unlocking it, staring down at the contents. He reached in and pulled out the photos of himself and his parents and then the journal that had been his grandfather's. It had been a while since he read it. Some thought in the back of his mind had him sitting back and reading through it, finally marking a spot. He glanced at the clock. It was too late in the evening to talk to Andrew, but he'd make time in the morning. He needed to be working on his sermon for the following Sunday and that would be a task, given what they had all been through.

He marked his spot and then returned the journal to the box, locking it away again. His thoughts turned to Madi, as he called her, and he smiled. She was a spitfire, he thought, but with compassion and caring ingrained in her personality. He was going to enjoy getting to know her, even though they would feel like they were under a microscope. He smiled as he remembered her fussing at him today about taking it easy. Yes, she was someone he wanted to get to know better. Lord, it's in Your hands. You know the reason she's in my life.

Madigan looked up from the desk work she was immersed in as she heard loud voices from the front of the building her parents owned. She rose, heading that way, when her mother appeared.

"Madigan. Come. Out the back with me. Now." Mary pulled her daughter with her, through the warehouse and garage to the back where she shoved her into her car and then slid behind the wheel.

"Mom?" Madigan stared at the building, then turned her eyes on her mother.

"Someone was in there asking for you. I finally got rid of him and locked the doors.

I didn't feel safe." Mary pulled out her phone to call for help. "Your Dad and brother aren't close enough to help us."

"Mom, what did he look like?" At her mother's description of the man, Madigan's head went back on the headrest and her eyes closed. "He sounds like the man from yesterday. What does he want with me?"

"He can't get back here, not with the fencing." Her mother's hands were shaking as she tried to call for help, finally finding the numbers.

Thirty minutes later, Madigan and Mary stood, watching as the officers walked through the building and around outside.

Bill Buckley, a detective on the force, stood beside them. "Madigan, do you think it was the same man you had the contact with yesterday?"

She shrugged. "I didn't see him today, but it could be. I just don't get why he'd be after me, not Silas. It was Silas he was after yesterday."

"But you're the one he tried to take with him, weren't you?" Bill stared at her until she reluctantly looked at him and nodded.

Mary gasped as she drew her daughter close. "You didn't tell me about that."

Madigan shrugged. "I guess I forget. There was so much else going on." She peeked around her mother at Bill, to find him watching the crime scene team pack up and leave. "Bill? Are you going to talk to Silas?"

He shrugged. "More than likely." He turned to face them. "Stay safe. Mary, you did right, what you did today. Madigan, be very careful if you're out on your own. It sounds as if this man is after you, possibly to get to Silas. I hear tell you're a couple now." He smirked as he walked away, waving a hand at her shout of outrage.

"Madigan? Is this true?"

"Is what true?" Madigan became very busy straightening the papers at the reception counter, refusing to look at her mother.

"You and Silas? Are you a couple?" Mary's hands reached to touch her daughter's, to still her movements.

Madigan shook her head. "I don't think so, Mom. At least...." Her voice died away. Her eyes raised to her mother's, wonder in them as she thought about how Silas looked at her and watched her. "He looks at me, Mom, as if I'm so important to him, as if I'm the only one in the place with him. I've never had that before."

Mary's eyes filled with tears as she hugged her daughter, knowing she was right with her comments. "I know, Mads. I know. Leave it with God, love. If he's the one, you'll know." She stepped back, her hands on her daughter's shoulders, then one finger reaching under Madigan's chin to raise her face so she could study it. "He looks at you that way, I know. Both your Dad and I have seen it. Go for dinner with him. Take it cautiously, as I know you will. Pray about it."

Madigan nodded, a movement outside catching her attention. She suddenly pushed her mother away and ran to lock the door. She was too late as the door was yanked open, pulling her outside with it. Strong arms surrounded her and a hand was clasped over her mouth as she was picked up and carried away, her struggles not releasing her or letting her get away. She could hear her mother's screams in the background as she was thrown into a vehicle, doors slamming shut behind her, and the vehicle accelerating from the parking lot at a high rate of speed. Her head hit metal as she rolled with the movement of the van and her eyes slid closed as she dropped down into darkness.

Mary's screams echoed through the building and the parking lot. She searched for her phone, frantically calling for help. This couldn't have just happened, she cried. Tears of fear and anger tracked down her face as she ran towards the road, trying desperately to track where the vehicle had gone.

Silas raised his head from the deep study he was in, preparation under way for his Sunday sermon, as he heard Anna's voice raised in alarm, then a knock at his door. He rose, opening it to find Andrew on the other side.

Andrew pointed into his office, and Silas stepped back to let him in and then closed the door, watching as Andrew paced for a few minutes, hands deep in his jacket pockets.

"Andrew?" Silas waited until Andrew turned back to face him. "Andrew? You're here for a reason, and somehow, I don't think it's me."

"It is, and it isn't." Andrew sighed, not quite knowing how to tell Silas. "Mary and Madigan were approached by a man who we think was the man from yesterday. Mary got rid of him, locked up the building and stuck Madigan into her car. After Bill had left, they were talking and Madigan heard a noise outside. Mary said she tried to lock the door but instead was abducted." Andrew watched with compassion as Silas' eyes slid closed. "We're looking for her now. Do you remember anything about the man?"

Silas shook his head. "No. Not really. Not him. It all happened so fast. But I did find this, on top of the piles of papers. I was heading your way later." He pulled out the paper he had picked up from the pile and handed it to Andrew. "This isn't mine. You can tell, it's not my handwriting. I have no idea whose it is."

Andrew reached for it, reading it over before he looked up at Silas. "I don't like this, Silas. This definitely makes you a target. Do you know this person, Jerry Lake?"

Silas shook his head. "I've never heard of him." He paused. "I was reading through my grandfather's journal and found something, a similar name. I need to show it to you, but it's at my home."

Andrew turned. "Come on, then. Can you leave your study and come with me?"

Silas nodded. "Anything to find Madi."

Andrew stopped him with a hand on his arm, his eyes searching his friend's face, his heart raised in prayer for her safe return. "Are you that serious about her, Silas?"

Silas stopped in his tracks, standing beside Andrew's car, his eyes fixed in the distance. "I am, Andrew. I think she's the missing half of my heart. Do you understand?" He turned to look at his friend, catching a look in his eyes and on his face that had him frowning.

Andrew nodded. "I do. It's how I feel about Phoebe." He pointed to the car. "Now, into that. Let's go find what you were talking about and then head for the department." He pulled away from the church. "Are you sure you have time for this?"

Silas nodded, not really hearing Andrew's voice, his thoughts on Madigan. Please, Lord, protect her. Bring her back home safely and soon. We all need her with us.

Madigan struggled against the bonds holding her to the pole she was tied to. She had awakened, her head pounding, her eyes blinking open and closed as she tried so hard to focus without success. She couldn't think where she was. She just knew she was in trouble and no one knew where she was. She finally managed to open her eyes and keep them open, scanning the room she was in. Her heart sank. She was in a basement, with small dirt-encrusted windows.

Dust, dirt and cobwebs adorned the basement. She was sitting on dirt, the floor above her just enough to clear her head. A crawlspace, she thought. She twisted and turned, pulling at her bonds without success. Tears tracked through the dirt on her face, leaving muddy trails. She rubbed at her shoulders to try and stop them, leaving marks on her T-shirt. Her head went back on the post, and her eyes sank closed. Lord, I have no idea where I am or who took me. I'm trusting that You do. I know You know exactly where I am and why I was taken. I'm scared and terrified and just want to go home. She sat like that for hours, it seemed, no one coming near her before she finally dozed off.

She roused hours later, just how many she wasn't sure. It was pitch black and she could hear rustling around her. She jerked and then shivered, not sure who or what she was sharing her space with. Her head turned as she struggled to see through the darkness, with what little moonlight filtered through the windows. She listened to the footsteps over her head, praying it was a rescuer, but knowing it was likely her kidnappers. How long had it been? She had lost track of time. Lord, she prayed, I need out of here and now. Why did You let this happen to me? I could have done without this, You know. She sighed, knowing that her prayer was futile in the short term. Lord, please bring someone to find me. I don't know how but You do.

She leaned her head back, trying to work up enough saliva to wet her mouth but couldn't. She heard the scraping of wood and saw light appear from the upstairs, blinding her as she was untied and pulled up to the main floor and shoved down into a chair. She shook from fear, not daring to raise her eyes to look at the men. She saw their dirty work boots and swallowed hard.

She couldn't understand what they were saying, her mind just not forming the words. She stared at the pen and paper in front of her, not recognizing what they were. She vaguely heard footsteps retreating and scraped up the courage to look up and then around. They were in another room. She rose, her feet silent on the floor, as she crept across the dusty floor, heading for the door and freedom. She reached for the knob, praying it would be unlocked, and pulled the door open, sliding it shut behind her. She stared around and then ran for the building behind the house and past there into the open field, racing as hard as she could for the rocks she could see in the distance. She heard shouts from the house and then she was in the rocks, seeking somewhere to hide.

She scrambled into the rocks, looking for anywhere she could fit into, finally finding a shelter behind a huge rock. She sunk into in, drawing up her legs and arms and burying her face. She prayed the men didn't see her.

She heard them run past, searching for her, and slunk even lower into the rocks, as low as she could. She waited, hearing them run back again, heading for the house. She didn't dare move, couldn't move, wouldn't let them know where she was.

Night gave way to dawn before she raised her head and listened. She was on her own but had no idea where she was. She crept from cover, her eyes seeking the men, her movements slow and cautious as she made her way out of the rocks and then turned in a circle, not quite sure which was to go, other than away from where the house lay. She swiped at her face, brushing away the tears again, before she put one foot in

front of the other and walked away, heading
where she didn't know.

Chapter 7

Silas sat on the church platform the next day, his eyes assessing his people, searching for the lady he knew wouldn't be there. He found Matthew, Mary, and Mitchell in their usual seat, four pews back from the front, and the empty spot between Mitchell and his mother tore at his heart. Lord, bring her home safely please. He fingered the note in his pocket. He needed to talk to Mitchell after church. He had an idea where Madigan might be.

He finally stood and approached the pulpit, his eyes on his notes before he raised them to the ceiling, nodding in confirmation. His deep bass voice filled the sanctuary as he spoke, stating he wasn't going to preach that day, that the time would be spent in prayer and praise, the people ministering to each other. He had a few frowns, a few raised eyebrows, and knew he would hear about this afterwards. But he was sure this was what God wanted that day, and God came first.

Mitchell walked towards Silas after the sanctuary had emptied, his hands jammed into his jeans pockets.

"Silas?" Mitchell stood, his eyes on the stained glass window behind the cross.

"Mitchell. No word?" At the negative shake of his friend's head, he pulled out the paper he had been fingering. "I had this on my door this morning."

Mitchell glanced at him, his hand stilling as he read. "On the Old School Road? The abandoned farm house at the very end?"

"I'm planning on going out there to check it out. Care to come along?"

Mitchell nodded. "I'll follow you to your place so you can change and grab what you need. Then we'll stop by my place and I'll grab my gear and let Dad know what's up and give him a timeline for when we'll be back."

Silas nodded as he set the alarm and locked the church doors. "Thanks, Mitchell. I pray this works out."

"You and me both, Silas." Mitchell stood for a moment, his eyes on the keys he has holding. "I'm not sure where you want to go with your friendship with Mads, but she needs someone like you." He turned and walked away, leaving Silas gaping after him before he slammed his mouth shut and walked rapidly to his car.

An hour later, the two men stood, matching in height and almost in build, staring at the house. "If she was here, we need to be careful not to disturb anything. Andrew will have our heads as it is for coming out here without him." Mitchell's heart sank as he took in the weathered building.

"I spoke with him, Mitchell, earlier this morning. He agreed we could come look around, just not go into the building if we didn't have to." He caught his friend's shoulder. "Let's pray before we go any further."

Mitchell walked around to the back of the building as Silas approached the front, hoping to find any clue, no matter how small, to show that Madigan had been there. Silas studied the prints he was following, two men and a woman, he thought. He cupped his hands to look into the windows, moving from one to the other, seeing the disturbance on the floor. He dropped off the porch and then to his knees to stare into the crawl space window, his heart sinking as he saw the ropes lying on the dirt.

He rose, his phone in his hand, as he heard a shout from Mitchell and ran towards him.

"She was here, Silas, and heading that way." Mitchell pointed away from the house. "Let's get our packs and we can go."

"I don't know anything about tracking." Silas stood, his eyes assessing the distance from the house to the rocky ridge.

"I have some knowledge. I've worked with the search and rescue before, still do when work allows."

Silas handed Mitchell his keys. "Grab mine, please. I'm going to let Andrew know what we've found." He waited until Mitchell disappeared before making the call.

"Silas? You're calling. Did you find something?" Andrew's voice held hope.

"She was here, Andrew. I can see ropes in the crawl space, but it looks as if she got free and is on the run. We're going after her."

Andrew tried to talk him out of it, finally sighing. "I'll send in my team and meet them there. Stay in touch."

Handing Silas his pack, Mitchell slid his over his shoulders and then stood for a moment. "Can we pray, Silas? We need guidance because I have no idea where to search."

"That we can do." Silas prayed as he had never prayed before, his audible voice seeking guidance and wisdom in their search, his inaudible words crying out to God to protect his lady as he now thought of Madigan.

Mitchell took the lead, his eyes on the ground, following the flight of the smaller footprints with the larger footprints sometimes covering them.

"She headed for those rocks, Silas. I just pray we find her and that they haven't."

"I don't think they have." Silas stood for a moment, his eyes on the ground. "I only see one set of prints heading away that are smaller, none heading back towards the house. Just the men's."

"Then we need to get going. I'm sure they'll be back at some point to look for her." Mitchell looked around the rocks, finally pointing. "This way. It looks as if she's walking away from the house."

Silas nodded, as he turned back to look at the house. "That makes sense. Let's see if we can find her." He shifted his backpack and set out after Mitchell, his eyes searching the area around him.

It was close to night when Mitchell held up his hand, his eyes focused on a clearing ahead of them. Silas moved to his side, a question on his face.

"There, I think. She's holed up around here somewhere."

"How do we find her without spooking her?" He searched the small clearing. "There. In the centre. There she is."

Mitchell stilled, his eyes on his sister, relief coursing through him. "I have no idea what to do now, Silas. Somehow, I don't think we're going to be able to walk right up to her."

Silas shook his head. "I doubt it." He looked around, finally pointed. "Let me make my way around to the other side. I'll come in behind her to keep her from running that way. By the looks of the area, she can only come this way or go that way."

Mitchell blew out a breath, knowing it was the only way. "I guess. Do you have cell service?"

Silas pulled out his phone. "Not real great. Let me send off a text to Andrew. Whereabouts are we?"

"Let him know we're in White's Woods, near the old mill."

Silas pocketed his phone, then with a quick clasp to Mitchell's shoulder, strode away, heading for the other side of the clearing.

Mitchell watched as Silas stepped through the tall grass and shrubs and then stopped, dropping his pack to the ground and moving a few feet closer to Madigan, his eyes on her. Lord, let this work, please. Let me get my sister home. Mitchell stepped into the clearing, dropping his pack as well as he moved carefully and cautiously towards his sister.

"Mads? Madigan? It's Mitchell." He watched in shock as she looked up, then scrambled backwards from him, bringing her feet under her ready to run, her head shaking the whole time. "Mads? It's me."

He reached out to lightly grasp her arms, to keep her from moving further away. She gave a low scream, then fought him, her hands flying as she struggled against his light grasp. A blow caught him on his cheek, causing him to drop her one arm and she wrenched the other one from him, backing away, a look of outright fear on her face, her whole body shaking.

Madigan was more frightened than she had been, even when she ran the night before. They had found her again, those two men, and who knew what they would do to her. She vaguely remembered them asking her to do something but her mind refused to bring it forward. She kept backing away, fear driving her, until she backed into someone. She stood frozen, hands and arms raised, eyes on the ground.

Silas staggered a bit from the force Madigan had hit him with, then stood still, waiting for what he wasn't quite sure. He watched as Mitchell stood, fists clenched as his side, a look of agony on his face as his sister backed away from him and safety. She stood, not moving away, shudders running through her body, her pulse racing, her breath coming in gasps. He finally started speaking softly, his bass voice rumbling in her ear.

Mitchell watched and waited, knowing that Silas was speaking to Madigan, even though he couldn't hear the words.

Silas quoted verses about comfort and safety, prayed, and then began to hum, words of hymns coming to his lips as he sang in a low voice. He could finally feel her start to relax against him and brought his arms around her, hands palm up and in front of her. She finally reached to touch his hands, lightly laying hers on his, ready to pull them back. He waited, not caring how long it took for her to feel safe. She finally gripped his hands and with that, he knew she felt safe. Holding on to her hands, he wrapped his arms around her, his chin on her head, still humming quietly. She finally struggled to release her hands, turning to wrap her arms around him, her head against his chest, his heart thumping under her ear.

Mitchell approached, tears he didn't even know he had been shedding on his cheeks. "Thank you, Silas. Now, can we get her sitting down?" He took one of the thin metallic thermal blankets and spread it out near a tree. "Can you sit with her, Silas, at least for a bit?"

Silas nodded, his arms around the most precious bit of humanity he felt he had ever held, and worked to walk her over to the blanket. He released her enough to draw her down with him, wrapping her back into his arms when he was done, her head cradled on his shoulder.

"Now what, Silas?" Mitchell sank to the ground in front on them, his eyes on his sister's mud-streaked face, at the vacant stare. She had withdrawn to somewhere he didn't know how to reach.

"We'll need to wait, Mitchell." Silas squinted at the sky. "It's too late to try and walk her out of here tonight. Is it safe enough, do you think, to start a small fire and heat some water?"

Mitchel shrugged. "I have no idea but I think we should be okay. We're miles from that old farm house." He rose, his eyes on his friend, his mouth opening and closing before he shook his head and walked away, searching for wood for a fire. He agreed. They would need it before night was through.

"Mitchell, if you can heat some water, I'll like to try and clean her face and hands. I can feel a cut on one I think we need to look at." Silas hadn't taken his eyes from Madigan's face, missing the speculative look Mitchell shot him.

Mitchell finally brought the small pot of warm water and a rag he had stuffed into his pack over. "How do you want to do this?"

"I think she'll let me do her face, and then we'll work on her hands." He took the warm wet rag and tilted his head to watch Madigan, speaking softly and gently to her. He laid the cloth on her face, waiting as she winced and pulled back, her head hitting his shoulder before she stilled and let him wash the mud and traces of tears from her face. He handed Mitchell the cloth. "I'll hold her hands if you wash them. I think it might take two of us to manage that."

Mitchel agreed. "Which one has the deepest cut?"

"Her right hand."

"I'll start with the left. You may have to do this. She might not let me." He stared at his friend. "What did they do to her, Silas?"

Silas was silent for a moment. "I have no idea, Mitchell. Whatever happened, it terrified her. I haven't seen anything this bad in a long time."

Mitchell sat back on his heels, his eyes on his sister. "You've seen something like this?"

Silas nodded, his gaze finally meeting Mitchell. "At the youth home I worked at during seminary. We have a pair of brothers come in, totally shut down like this. We never did find out why. It took months to get them to where they were almost normal."

"Months?" Mitchell let out a low whistle.

"I don't think it will take that long with her. They had been abused or whatever for years." He looked down at the hand Mitchell was cleaning, wincing at the depth of the cut. "I doubt it will be like that for her. She was only there for a short while."

Mitchell didn't respond as he set butterfly bandages over the cut and then wrapped it tight. "She needs stitches. We have to get her out of here."

"And we will, just not tonight." Silas looked around, then down at Madigan. "I need to lay her down and I'm not sure she'll let me." He felt her beginning to shiver with the cold and moved away from her enough to shrug out of his jean jacket and slip it on her. "Madi, I'm going to lay you down on this nice blanket. It will keep you warm." She clutched his hand tight enough hers turned white. "It's okay. I'm not going anywhere, not too far. You need to sleep, okay, sweetheart? Here, down you go."

Mitchell watched as Silas worked with his sister, wishing she had let him help her, but knowing if he tried she would likely run and who knows where they would find her. Silas finally stepped back after wrapping the blanket around her, rubbing his hands up and down his arms.

Mitchell dug through his pack, then turned to Silas', pulling out a fleece sweatshirt Silas had packed and handing it to him. He watched as Silas absentmindedly slipped it on, finger combing his hair back into place before he turned to his friend.

"Any chance of coffee?"

Mitchell nodded. "I only have instant but that will work." He walked away to the stream they had passed, rinsing out the pot before filling it with water. "This should be okay. I have some stuff to treat it."

Silas nodded as he sank to the ground, his eyes on Madigan. "How far do we need to walk out?"

"The mill is a couple of miles from here, but with limited cell service, I'm not sure Andrew will be there. We'll pass it on our way to the road. Once we're out of here, we'll have service again. The road is about five miles from here."

"Five miles, is it? I'm not sure Madi will make it that far." Silas prayed she would but he knew better.

"We'll get her out, Silas, even if we have to carry her." He smirked. "Sorry, I meant to say, even if you have to carry her."

Silas laughed, knowing Mitchell was joking. "And I would carry her many more miles than that to get her to safety."

adigan's eyes slid open the next morning as she stirred, dawn barely breaking over the horizon. She pulled the blanket up tighter, her fingers feeling at the material, before she stared at her bandaged hand. She frowned. The men chasing her wouldn't have helped her this way. She raised her head a few inches and looked around. She stilled as she saw the male figure sitting near a low fire, and another body wrapped up in a blanket, lying opposite her.

She sat up, pushing the hair from her face, pushing down the fear she had been kidnapped again, and searching for a way out. She started as the man sitting near the fire turned, then rose, dropping into a crouch a few feet away from her, his eyes searching her face. She kept her eyes down, not on him. She finally reached to take his hand he was holding out, feeling the strength and kindness in his grip, not hearing the words he was speaking, and let him pull her to her feet. He walked her to the entrance to the clearing, pointing off to the side before he retreated, standing with his back to her. She stared at him for a moment before heading into the woods.

Silas sighed. She was still not responding to him like she should. He walked over and nudged Mitchell, who roused, sitting up and then springing to his feet when he didn't see Madigan.

"She's fine, Mitchell. She'll be right back." Silas stared down at the remnants of the fire, his thoughts going to what they faced on their walk out and what Madigan faced once she was safe.

Mitchel sighed. "No better?" When Silas shook his head, he turned to watch where Silas had pointed. "How do we reach her, Silas?"

"We won't until she feels absolutely safe. She doesn't out here. She's expecting the men to show up and take her away again." He turned as he heard her footsteps and walked towards her, stopping short of her, his hand outstretched. He waited until she decided he was safe and took his hand, leading her to the log he had been sitting on and drawing her down. "What would you like to drink, Madi? We have water or coffee." He waited, a smile lurking in his eyes. "Not choosing? How about water then?" He wrapped her hand around the metal cup and waited until she drank. "Now, we don't have much for breakfast, but I have a granola bar. Would you like one?" He held it out, but she refused to take it.

Mitchell snickered. "I should have warned you. She doesn't like granola bars." Silas stared at him, not quite sure he was serious. Mitchell shook his head. "She won't eat them. Says they taste like horse feed."

Silas watched as Mitchell packed up, then handed him his backpack before shouldering his own.

"Is she ready to move, Silas?" Mitchell's question was quiet.

Silas nodded and stood, holding out a hand to Madigan. She stared at it, before finally taking it and allowing him to pull her to her feet. He drew her with him, walking ahead of Mitchell, who pointed out the trail to take.

Hours later, they reached the road, Silas looking around for somewhere to let Madigan rest, finding a spot and gently drawing her down. He stood, his eyes searching the area around him. He could almost feel eyes on them.

Andrew stood beside his personal vehicle, his eyes on the three before he too searched the area. He walked towards them, his footsteps on the gravel road causing Madigan to sink back as far as she could into the tree and ground. He paused, his eyes on her, before he spoke.

"Mitchell? What's going on?"

"She's been like that since we found her, Andrew, withdrawn, not speaking. I can't get near her. The only one of the two of us who can reach her is Silas."

"That's interesting. So, you know nothing of what happened?"

Mitchell shook his head. "She hasn't spoken a word. I tried to reach out to her when we first found her and ended up with this bruise."

Andrew took a look at Mitchell's face, then back at Madigan. "Phoebe was like that when I rescued her. She had withdrawn to the point she wasn't speaking."

"Mads is like that. She won't look at us either." He looked over at his sister, worry and heartbreak on his face. "I just don't know how I'll explain it to Mom and Dad."

"Let's get her out of here and to the hospital to be assessed." Andrew paused as Mitchell laid a hand on his arm.

"She won't go, Andrew. Silas has been trying to talk her into that and she just refuses."

Andrew gave a sigh of frustration. "We need her to. Just to make sure she's okay. We also need it for the investigation." He looked over as Silas was helping Madigan into the back of his truck. "Can he talk her into it?"

"The only way would be if he stays with her and we know that won't happen at the hospital."

Andrew thought for a moment. "There's one way. I just don't know if Silas would go for it."

"And that would be?"

"If he's her husband. Then, he'd be able to stay."

Mitchell stared at him. "Are you serious?" After a moment, he continued. "You are serious."

"It's what happened with Phoebe and I. Silas convinced me that was the only way to keep her alive, and it turns out it was. This may well be the only way to do that with her.”

Mitchell stared at Silas as he stood at the open truck door, watching Madigan, before he slid in and closed the door.

“We may have to consider that. But who?”

“I’m heading for Riverville with you three. Let me have your truck keys and I’ll have someone meet us and grab your truck.” He took the proffered keys and pointed at the truck. “I’m not sure who I can trust right now. Riverville is a small town, but I have good friends there, including a pastor. I’ve talked to him already and he has paperwork ready to go.”

“You’re that sure?”

“I’m that hopeful, Mitchell. It’s not a light step. I’ve prayed hard about this.” He pointed to the truck. “And I can guarantee you that he has too.”

Silas stared at Andrew, then shook his head. “Throwing my words back at me, are you?” He shook his head again as Andrew grinned. “Do you really think it’s necessary?”

"I think so, Silas. If you're worried about the church, don't be. They'll understand."

"Not everybody." Mitchell's voice was low but the men with him caught his words.

"What do you mean, Mitchell?" Andrew shot him a glance.

"Warren Davis. He won't. He's been trying to find something to get rid of Silas and he'll use this."

"The board is about ready to kick him off, if you ask me. This would do it." Andrew shot a look over his shoulder at Madigan, who sat, wrapped in Silas' arm, her eyes down, her head on his shoulder. "I don't think we have many options here, Silas."

Silas watched as Andrew pulled into the hospital in Riverville, then reached to unfasten Madigan's seatbelt in careful motions before helping her from the truck, her hand tucked safely in his.

The three men stood outside the examination room, waiting, Silas' eyes glued to the door, not seeing the man approaching Andrew. Sudden noise and the clanging of metal drew him to the door and he was through it, Mitchell on his heels, desperately seeking Madigan.

The nurses and doctor stood for a moment before one of the nurses reached to pull Madigan to her feet from the corner she was crouched in, arms over her head. A whimper came from her, breaking the hearts of the two men who loved her. Mitchell nodded at Silas who moved in, asking the nurse to step aside.

He crouched in front of Madigan, his voice low and soft, speaking words of comfort to her, before she lowered her arms and reached for him. He cradled her close before he stood, heading for the examination table. She refused to sit on it, not until he sat beside her, an arm around her. She still flinched with each touch or word from the others.

Andrew stepped back out into the hall with Mitchell and finally approached the man who had appeared.

"Greg! Good to see you. The family's well?"

"We're doing well, Andrew. Phoebe is too?" Greg Evans was the pastor of the church in Riverville. "I can see what you mean, Andrew. What can I do?"

"You have the paperwork I asked about?"

"I do. The clerk was glad to help out. Have you convinced them yet?"

Andrew shook his head. "Not yet. But you can see that she'll only let him around her. I don't think even her mother would be able to touch her right now."

Silas stepped from the room, his eyes turning back to watch Madigan, who had her eyes fastened on him, a fearful look on her face. "What caused this, Andrew?"

"Fear can do it."

Mitchell groaned, his head going back against the wall he was leaning on. "I never thought. I never connected the two."

"Connected what?" Silas spoke for the three men with Mitchell.

"She has an absolute terror of the dark. It started when she was young. She can't explain it. She was fine. Then when she was about ten something happened, she's never said what, and to this day she can't handle total darkness. It shuts her down, but I've never seen her like this. Usually she's up and around again in no time."

Silas sighed, his eyes meeting Andrew's. "They had her tied up in the crawlspace of the house, Andrew. That's why she's like she is."

Mitchell nodded. "I never made the connection about that, but then I didn't know she had been tied up down there for that long." He turned to where he could see Madigan, watched as she shook from fear and stress. He heard Silas give a low cry and then walk back into the room to sit beside her and wrap an arm around her and watched as Madigan leaned into him.

"Greg? Your thoughts?"

"What has Silas said?"

"He didn't get an opportunity to say much but I know he's thinking about it." Andrew turned with a frown as he felt watched, seeing no one close.

"What about your board? Will they accept this? Would your church or would they ask him to leave?"

"He'd leave if it meant keeping her safe." Andrew was sure of this. "I talked to our board chairman. He called me back a while ago. All but one are behind him. If Silas does go ahead with this, they plan on reaching out to the members and canvassing them."

Mitchell nodded. "Silas is well thought of and loved by our congregation. I can see very few not backing him." He nodded towards the door. "Here they come. Let's find somewhere we can talk. I don't think Mads can handle too many more new places."

"No, she can't. Let's find the chapel. It's this way." Greg led the way, stopping for a moment as he laid his hand on the door, asking for wisdom and guidance.

They sat, Mitchell on one side of his sister, Silas on the other. She looked up briefly at Andrew and then at Greg, before focusing her eyes on her hands.

Madigan struggled with the darkness that overwhelmed her. She wanted free, was crying out for God to release her, but she wasn't. She knew Mitchell was hurt because she wouldn't, couldn't turn to him. He didn't know the threats against her family that had driven to this darkness. Just like all those years ago. Those threats had seemed so real at that time. She felt Silas' hand on hers and she turned her hand, their fingers interlocking. She felt safe and at peace with him. But would they threaten him too?

She finally understood what the men were talking about and listened more fully. Her heart rose in hope. Was this was God had planned? Was this was He wanted for her? Silas was a good man, a man of God. She knew she could trust him, but would it be fair to him?

She heard his words, felt him turn so he could look at her brother, heard his declaration of love for her. She sighed, her head going down to rest on his shoulder. When questioned, she nodded, agreeing to what they asked.

Silas watched her face, saw the struggles she was going through, and then nodded himself. He drew her to her feet and to the front of the chapel, Mitchell by her one side, Andrew on the other side of Silas as Greg spoke the words that made them man and wife. She sighed to herself. This is not how she pictured herself getting married, but she knew it was God's plan for her.

Silas stood for a moment, his eyes on his new wife, realizing that they had had no rings to exchange. He stared at his hands, finally pulling off his grandmother's wedding band he wore on his right pinkie finger, praying that it would fit.

"Madi, this was my Grandmom's. She would be honoured if you would wear it for now."

Greg spoke up. "I forget, in all the fuss and bother, that Mary bought these for you two. If you don't want them, that's fine." He held out a hand with two rings on it that he had dug out of his pocket.

Silas picked up the lady's ring, intent on putting in on Madigan's finger, until she closed her hand. He sighed. Not that one, he thought. He then picked up the man's ring, hesitation in his movements, until she reached for it and slid it on his finger. He had hope then that she was starting to come around.

A few moments later, Andrew had hustled them out and to his truck. He could feel the eyes on them, had seen men watching them, and wanted them out of there as soon as he could get them out.

Mitchell stood for a moment, his eyes on his sister. "Silas, I need to talk to Mom and Dad. I don't know if they'll understand."

Silas nodded. "Send them to me when you have." He looked around. "Andrew, I don't feel safe taking Madi home tonight, not until you've made arrangements at my place. Where can we go?"

Greg spoke up. "We have an apartment over our garage. You're more than welcome to use it. I have friends who can watch out for you if we need to."

The men stood and watching, trying to determine exactly what was going on and how Madigan had made it back to her brother. They didn't know the other men she was with. They lost sight of them briefly, then saw her brother in a truck. They ran for their vehicle, determined to find her once more, not realizing that she was not there, that she and Silas had gone with Greg.

Chapter 9

*W*ith a quiet word of thanks to Mary and Greg, Silas shut the door of the apartment, his hand resting on the door as he set the lock, listening to their steps descend the stairs. He looked up, a strain showing around his eyes, as he questioned if he had done right by Madigan, if there had been some other way to protect her. He sighed, knowing that in his humanness, he had made a decision, feeling confident that it was the one God had led him to.

He turned, searching the apartment for his bride. He stopped in his tracks. His bride. How would the church react? He searched his mind for a new occupation he could undertake, knowing full well that being a pastor was who he was. He found Madigan sitting on the bed, her hands folded in her lap, fatigue weighing her down. He reached for her hand, pulling her to her feet before gently guiding her to the bathroom.

"Here, sweetheart. Get cleaned up. Mary left some clothes for you, brand new ones she said. She went shopping for you when Greg called her. You're safe. Go on."

Madigan finally made the move she needed, her eyes raising to Silas, who watched her intently before reaching forward to drop a kiss on her cheek. She nodded, closing the door behind her, feeling the clothes Mary had brought her, and then the thick fluffy towels. Tears sprang to her eyes, and she swiped at them angrily. As she dressed once more and brushed her wet hair, she made a determination. She was done running. She had been running for years and she was over that. Silas would help her. Lord, I need to talk and I just can't find the spoken word, not just yet. Please, Lord, let me speak.

Silas had stood, leaning against the wall until he heard the water running, then walked away, heading for the kitchen and coffee. Mary had said the kitchen was stocked. He peeked into the fridge. Good, food, he thought. His phone chimed and he searched for where he had left it, finally finding it on the dresser top where he had emptied his pockets.

"Silas?" He sighed as he heard Madigan mother's voice.

"Mary? I'm sorry." His words were cut off by her voice

"Silas, don't apologize. Mitchell talked to us. Welcome to the family, Silas. I just wish it had been different." He could hear the suppressed sob in her voice, and his heart broke. "Just keep our girl safe, please?"

"I will do my best, Mary, you can count on that. When this is all over, I want to redo this. Start planning what you want to do for her."

He could hear his mother-in-law's sobs and then Matthew had the phone. "Silas? Are you two okay for now?"

"We are. I'm not sure what Andrew has in mind, but I need to be back for Sunday." He sighed. "I'm just not sure how the church will react."

Matthew gave a low laugh. "You're not the first one of our church who has faced this and won. I would suspect very few will question you. We'll deal with them. You've always been there for anyone in the church. It's your turn to receive."

A few more words with Matthew and then he clicked off his phone, heading back to the bedroom. Madigan stood, staring at the bed, before raising her eyes to Silas.

He pulled back the covers. "Slide in, Madi. You need sleep. Do you want anything to eat first?"

She shook her head, opened her mouth to speak, and then frowned. He hugged her before tucking her in. He lay beside her, pulling her close to him, and watched and listened as her breathing evened out and she slept. He finally rose, heading for the kitchen and the coffee he had made, then changed his mind and headed for the shower instead.

He absentmindedly stirred his coffee as he listened to Andrew.

"We're fine, Andrew. Yes, Madi's asleep. What have you learned?"

Andrew sighed, knowing Silas wouldn't rest until he heard the news. "The body in the church? It's Jerry Lake. I have no idea how that paper ended up in your office, unless the killer dropped it."

"How old was he?"

"A few years older than us. Why?"

"Because something happened when Madi became afraid of the dark, and I think he's involved somehow. I'm going to try and find out from her but can you check him out? See what he's been up to?"

"I can do that. What day were you wanting to head back?"

"Today's Monday. How about Thursday?"

"I'll have someone pick you up. Bill's looking at upgrading the security on your home. Nothing overboard but you need it."

"Thanks, Andrew." Silas caught himself in the middle of a yawn. "I'll catch up with you tomorrow. And thanks for what you did."

"I can never repay you for what you did for Phoebe and myself. Take care. We're praying for you."

Silas stood staring down at his phone before reaching to turn off the coffee pot and empty it and reset it for morning, a habit he had. He turned, leaving low lights on throughout the apartment before stopping in the bedroom doorway. He sighed, knowing that he wouldn't be getting a lot of sleep that night, not likely, not when he felt he had to keep watch. He reached for a blanket, stretching out on top of the covers and drawing the blanket over him. He searched Madigan's face in the dim light, frowning as he saw the peace reflected there. His eyes closed and he slept.

❀ ❀ ❀ ❀

Stirring early the next morning, Madigan shifted in bed, feeling relaxed for the first time in days, she thought. She frowned as she opened her eyes, a panic setting in as she realized she wasn't in her own bedroom. She turned over quickly in bed and stopped, her eyes growing round, before she caught the glint on her finger and remembered what had transpired over the last few days. She studied Silas as he slept, seeing the shadows under his eyes, the stress showing in the lines of his face even as he slept. Lord, I have no idea where You're taking us, but it seems as it is through the fire and flood, now doesn't it? Couldn't we have just skipped all that? Guess not.

She slipped from bed, grabbing fresh clothes and dressing quickly, and then headed for the kitchen, stopping at the coffee pot. She smiled. Silas had set the coffee already. A man after her own heart. She rummaged through the fridge, finding plenty for breakfast. She paused, her hand on the fridge door, a carton of eggs in her other hand, as her eyes sought the door to the bedroom. She had no idea what Silas liked to eat.

Silas reached for Madigan as he awoke, finding emptiness on the bed. He shot up, frantic to find her, standing in the kitchen doorway, watching as she worked away before she turned, a small hesitant smile on her face as their eyes met.

"Good morning. Did you sleep well?" Silas watched as her mouth worked, trying to get out the words. He reached for her, drawing her close, before he prayed for healing for her.

She finally pushed away, her eyes on his face. She swallowed, her lips moving as she finally forced words out. "I did." Her eyes slid closed as the tears sparkled on her cheeks.

"Oh, sweetheart! You spoke!" He cradled her close, his head on hers as his tears wet her hair. "God is good, Madi. Now, let me get dressed, you finish breakfast, we'll eat and then talk." He turned to walk away before he spun to face her. "I meant every word yesterday. I do love you, more today than yesterday."

He walked away, leaving her staring after him, her mouth open, before she snapped it closed and turned back to the meal. She smiled. She was loved and she loved him back. What more could she ask for?

Silas set his phone down, not liking the conversation he had had with Andrew, and knowing he had to speak with Madigan. Their conversation had been quiet over the breakfast meal, just getting to start to know one another. He looked up as he felt her eyes on him and stood, reaching for her hand to lead her into the living room. Once seated, he prayed as he had never prayed before.

"Madi, they've identified the body in the church. It's Jerry Lake." Her body stiffened beside him. "Is he the one who scared you all those years ago, that made you afraid of the dark?"

She finally nodded, swiping at the tears on her face. "He is. I was ten, coming home from school, when he grabbed me and locked me into a shed that was pitch black. He wouldn't let me out, no matter how much I cried or screamed. He just kept saying he was told to do that. I don't remember much of what happened. I guess I shut down. All I could hear was some creatures moving around and all I could see was black. I have no idea how I got out of that shed or who helped me that day. Someone did. They cleaned me up, fed me and then watched me as I walked home." She looked up at him. "I hate the dark, the pitch blackness of it."

"I know." Silas drew her to him, his arms tight around her. "Andrew's looking into his past, and it's not pretty. He's been involved in a lot of petty thefts and drugs. Not so much in Elmton, but in Oak City. He ran with a pretty fast group in high school, didn't he? Andrew will figure it out." He waited for her to speak. "He's also tracking who owns the farm house you were held in. It's a numbered company, he said, and Bill is working through the layers of that."

She nodded, her hair brushing against his cheek. "I'm glad I can finally talk about it. I couldn't say anything to my parents or Mitchell. I can remember them being threatened, but it wasn't Jerry's voice who did that. It was an older voice, and I can't remember if it was a man or a woman."

"What do you mean?"

"What I said. It was either a man with a higher-pitched voice or a woman with a low voice. That's the problem. I never knew who to fear."

Silas sat for a while, his heart breaking for his bride, his thoughts lifting in prayer. "We'll make it a matter of prayer, sweetheart, that Andrew and his team can solve this. Now, we're stuck here today. What would you like to do? Andrew's agreed to pick us up Thursday."

She shrugged. "I have no idea. Is it safe for us to go out?"

"I don't see why not. No one should know we're here." He reached for her hand. "Are you sure about Grandmom's ring?"

"I am. I'm honoured to wear it. But what about yours?" She frowned as she fingered the ring. "It's definitely not what I would have chosen for you."

"Then, sweetheart, that's what we'll do. We'll find the jewelry store in town and you can buy me a new ring." He grinned at the look on her face. "And I can buy you the engagement ring I should have." He stopped, his eyes searching her face. "I don't like how we had to do this, but I love that you're mine."

She nodded, her eyes on the far wall. "Mom and Dad must feel so cheated."

"I talked to them last night, and we'll call them this afternoon, okay? They understand, sweetheart. Besides, I told your Mom that when this was all over, we'd redo our wedding and she could start planning it now."

She groaned. "You really didn't, did you? Now, look what you've done. You've loosed my mother on the world."

Silas laughed unrepentantly as he drew her to her feet, found jackets for them, and then locked the door behind them, tucking her close to his side, not seeing Greg and Mary watching them walk away. "No, she'll be good. I trust her."

She snorted. "You have no idea what you've done, do you? I'll have to sit hard on her, to keep it simple."

"You want simple? Then tell her that. If you don't, I will."

She nodded, her eyes searching the town, liking what she say. "I like this town, Silas. We need to come back and explore it." She stopped in front of a bakery. "An Irish bakery? Oh, we need to stop here on the way back. Mom makes some of the recipes her mother brought with her. I would love to have some of these."

Silas laughed. "We can do that. Let's move on though first. I'm not quite hungry yet."

She laughed at his nonsense, even as her eyes found a man standing watching them. Her laughter died but Silas didn't notice, intent on finding that jewelry store.

Two hours later, Madigan stood in the Irish bakery, her mouth watering as she looked over the selection of baked goods.

"What do I start with, Silas?" She had become more comfortable with him over the morning.

"What appeals to you?" He looked up with a smile at the woman around their age who stood behind the counter. "Perhaps you can recommend something?"

She nodded. "That I can. Are you familiar with Irish baking?"

Madigan gave a happy nod. "I am. Silas, I still don't know what to choose."

Rylee Allison laughed as she looked up to the opening door. "Dave, love. How come you're here? I thought you were working?"

Her husband came around and greeted her. "I got sent home. Something about too much overtime. And who do we have here?"

Madigan looked up, her eyes meeting Dave's, realizing he had been the one watching her.

"I'm Silas Peters, pastor in Elmton, and this is my bride, Madigan."

"I'm Dave and this is my wife, Rylee." Dave looked around. "Do you have time for coffee or tea?"

Silas nodded. "We do. We're here for the day, heading back home Thursday. Did you decide, sweetheart?" He watched her face for a moment. "Madi, did you decide?"

"Oh, what? Yes, some of those cookies please and a pasty I think."

"A pasty? Don't think I'm familiar with those." Silas laughed at the look on her face.

Later, Dave drew Silas aside on a pretext. "Listen, Andrew called our police chief. Caleb spoke with me. Andrew wanted you warned that the men after you are searching the towns around here and they likely hit this town as well."

Silas stared at him, then sighed. "I guess that means we go back to the apartment then."

"Not necessarily. I have friends I can take you to, or you can come stay with us for the rest of the day. Rylee's usually done by two and it's almost that now. I would say our ladies have hit it off." He nodded towards them. "One thing you need to know. Madigan saw me watching you two earlier, trying to think of a way to approach you."

"Does your chief do this often, use people other than his own men?"

"Under certain circumstances, he will." Dave motioned towards Rylee. "We had our own adventures as have had many of our friends. We know somewhat of what you're facing."

Chapter 11

On Thursday evening, Silas hesitated for a moment, then swept Madigan into his arms, carrying her into the house, against her protests. He laughed as he set her down.

"You've never been here, I don't think, Madi, and that's not right. Go on, look around all you want. I'll bring in our stuff." He stood for a moment watching the emotions playing across her face, then nodded as he turned. He had forgotten Madigan had walked through it with him when he couldn't remember who he was.

Madigan walked slowly through the downstairs of the old home that Silas had lovingly restored, seeing it with different eyes now that it was her home. She stopped in his office, her hand resting on his chair, knowing this was where he spent time in spiritual battle. She prayed for him and for them both.

She turned as she heard his footsteps. "I like your home, Silas."

He smiled. "I've spent time fixing it up. It was in rough shape when I bought it."

He held out a hand. "Come on. Let's do the rest of the tour and then see if I have anything left in the fridge that's edible."

She nodded, sudden shyness overtaking her. "How many bedrooms are there?"

"Three and each has its own bathroom. I set it up that way for comfort's sake for guests."

"That's a nice thought."

Silas turned as he heard the doorbell. "Must be Andrew. He said he'd be by tonight."

Andrew finally reached for Phoebe's hand, drawing her with him. He nodded to Silas. Their talk had not gone well. Andrew didn't have a lot of news to share, and Silas was frustrated. He wanted Madigan safe, now, and that didn't appear that it would happen.

Madigan watched from the kitchen doorway as Silas paced. "Silas? What did Andrew have to say?"

"Not a lot. He has no new leads. The house revealed nothing. You can't remember who took you. That's about the sum of it. He said if they couldn't find anything new in the next couple of days, they would have to set it aside."

She nodded. "That's what I expected. Now, what are we to do? We haven't talked about what we should or shouldn't do, whether I keep working or not."

Silas reached to hug her. "We can talk in the morning. I have to go by the church. I'd like you to come with me. Do you want to keep working?"

She hesitated before she replied. "I'm not sure any more. At one time, I would have said absolutely. Now, with you, I'm not so sure. Being a pastor's wife is something I never ever considered."

"You'll be a great one. We just need to watch that you don't get pulled into everything that's going on and every committee that's out there."

Friday morning, Silas turned from his church office phone, not seeing Madigan, but hearing her voice talking with Anna. He smiled. She would do okay, he thought, a prayer raised for guidance and wisdom for her. He turned back to his study, working on Sunday's sermon, losing himself to time and surroundings.

He felt a touch on his shoulder and looked up. Madigan stood there, watching him.

"It's after three, Silas. You have't had any lunch."

He was surprised. "It's that late? What have you done with yourself all day?" He rose and swooped in to kiss her, liking her surprise.

"I spent the day with Anna, getting to know the church and the programs and the people. You have a wonderful congregation, Silas."

He looked down at his desk, tidying his papers and locking them away before reaching for her hand. "That we do, sweetheart. They're your people too, you know. Now let's say I take my bride out for dinner."

"Is it safe, do you think?"

He shrugged. "We have to continue to live, Madi. We can't live in fear. And just maybe us being out and about will draw them out of wherever they're hiding and we'll get this over with."

"I'm afraid, Silas." She waved at Anna as they walked out. "I'm afraid of what's coming."

"I am too, but that's where our trust in God comes in. He knows what's ahead and He has prepared us for it and prepared those who will help us."

Silas glared down at his plate as they sat in Ev's diner, a local restaurant they both enjoyed eating in. Madigan gave a soft laugh, and he looked up at her in frustration.

"Eat while you can, Silas. Before someone else comes to congratulate you. I didn't realize how well thought of you are."

He finally sighed and picked up his hamburger, staring at it. "I should have taken you out of town, sweetheart. Then we could have eaten in peace."

Madigan shook her head and he sent her a questioning look. "It's okay, Silas. Really it is. I think's it's kind of cute how they're checking us both out."

He stared at her, then stared to laugh. "They are, aren't they?" He froze. "And here comes trouble."

Dean Adams stood staring at the two of them. "I heard you got hitched, Silas. I'm surprised it was so quick. There must have been a reason." His innuendo brought Silas to his feet, his fists clenched.

"That is enough of that, Dean. You are a way out of line here." He looked past him. "I glad you don't represent the board's feelings."

"Who says I don't?" His arrogance steamed from him.

Silas nodded behind him. "Art Wayne for one."

Dean struggled to control his rage. "We'll see about that." He stormed away, leaving the three of them staring after him.

Art shook his head. "I think he's done on the board now, Silas. This is the last straw with him. He's been warned so many times."

Silas nodded, then spoke with Art at length, his eyes finally resting on Madigan. "Thanks for the support, Art. I think I need to finish my meal with my wife."

"That you do. Welcome to the family, Madigan. I know you'll be a welcome addition." He nodded and walked off.

Madigan stared after him, then at Silas. "Is he for real?"

Silas laughed. "He is. Are you through or do you want something more?"

"I think I would like to go home, Silas. It's been a long day."

He nodded and reached for her hand, not seeing the smiles and nods as they walked out, and also not seeing the danger that lurked in the shadows.

Sunday morning found Madigan pacing Silas' office at the church as he finished off what he needed to do before he looked up at her, crossing to hug her.

"You're worried, aren't you?" At her nod, he hugged her tighter. "It's scary when you're first presented, but it does get easier."

"That's okay for you to say. You do this all the time."

He laughed and ducked the slap she playfully aimed at him. "Let's pray, sweetheart. Then I, no we, need to meet with the team for prayer."

Silas drew a deep breath and reached for Madigan's hand, feeling hers trembling in his as they walked towards the sanctuary. He deliberately walked in so he was between the congregation and his wife, his eyes focused on the platform before he frowned. The church board and the deacons and all the wives stood waiting for him. Then he heard the clapping, and turned, his mouth dropping open before he clamped it shut. He felt Madigan's step falter.

Art stepped forward and motioned for them both to come up on the platform. Silas stopped, his arms going around Madigan as she stood in front of him, her hands finding his. Little did they know that movement endeared them even more to their people.

"Silas. Madigan. Welcome home. It's a great pleasure for us to have both of you up here today. No long speeches. We just wanted to welcome you home, welcome Madigan as your helpmeet, Silas, and to pray for you both. We know your battle is far from over and we want to wrap you in prayer."

Silas walked Madigan down to the front pew where her parents and brother were waiting and then looked up. His friends had gathered around them in the front pews. He sighed. He didn't realize how many friends he had.

He stood after church, his arm around Madigan as the last of the people walked away. He could tell she was tired by the way she leaned on him.

Andrew and Phoebe stood watching, Phoebe's eyes on Madigan, Andrew assessing them both and then assessing the area around them. He could feel the eyes, could feel the danger, the evil, but couldn't see anyone. Who was it, Lord? I know they're here in the church, but who is it?

Madigan watched as the man crossed the parking lot, a frown on her face, before she felt for Silas' hand. "He's here, Silas. There, in the parking lot. I'm sure that's one of them."

Silas watched as the man walked off down the street, before he turned catching Andrew's eye, who nodded and then spoke to Phoebe. They walked to Andrew's truck, and Andrew drove way, following the path of the man.

"Andrew will find out what's up with him and track him down if he needs to. Now, let's get you home."

"Mom wants us to come for a meal."

"Do you want to? It's up to you and how you feel. You've had a very rough week."

She nodded. "I would like to. If you do."

"Madi, never question if I want to see your family. I'm glad to have a mom and dad and brother. I've been on my own for so long I'm glad. Mom and Dad are away on the mission field so much I feel like I'm an orphan."

She nodded. "If it's okay, I think I would rather just go home. I need to sleep, and then we need to make some decisions."

He frowned and then turned to lock up the church, catching her hand to walk to his vehicle. He stopped, shutting the door behind her, his eyes raised as he felt the evil approaching.

Madigan stopped beside Silas as he stood on his back deck, her eyes searching his face. "Silas, we need to talk about me working. I'm not sure how you feel."

He turned, pulling her over to the swing. "It's up to you, sweetheart, if you do or not. There'll be things you'll want to get involved in at church, but I don't want you to overdo it."

She nodded, then looked around. "He's out there, Silas. I can feel him. When will we be safe?"

He nodded. "I know. I hate living like this. I pray it's over soon." He looked down at her, then smiled. "They took me by surprise this morning. I never expected that."

"You're loved by your church, Silas. It shows." She hesitated before speaking further. "I just pray that whoever is after me doesn't spoil this for you."

"I don't think they will." He turned her back to the house. "How about some tea or coffee and some of that cake that was dropped off earlier?"

She nodded. "Sounds good, Silas. Thank you for being who you are."

Chapter 12

The man hunkered down in the shrubs lining the back of Silas's yard, watching for an opportunity. She lived here now and it should be easy to snatch her. She came out on her own a lot. He grinned in malicious, vicious glee. Soon, she would be his again, his to torment and terrify. He just had to be patient.

Silas stepped out onto the back deck in the early morning light, a frown on his face. He felt watched and from somewhere close. He searched and saw nothing. He knew someone was there. He turned and looked back at the house, knowing Madigan was still asleep. He turned back, catching a flash of movement, and frowned, then walked towards the back of the yard, his eyes alert. He stopped short of the shrubs, trying to place where he had seen the movement, then shrugged, walking back to the house.

The hand that came out to grab him withdrew as the man cursed softly. He had almost had him. If he had taken him down, then he could have made it into the house and got her. Another day, another try. He stepped back, careful not to leave a trail.

Madigan met Silas at the door, a frown on her face. "You're worried."

"I am, Madi. Something was off in the backyard. It's likely a good idea that you don't go out there without me for now, until we catch these guys."

She nodded. "I won't. Now about today. What are you up to?"

"I normally take Mondays off. What's your schedule?"

"Well! How do you like that? I just so happen to be off on Mondays too." She grinned at his look of pleasure. "So, what will we do with today?"

"Why don't we grab some of your stuff from your Mom's and you can start making our house a home." He hugged her. "Thank you, Madi." Then his head lowered as he thoroughly kissed his wife.

Andrew turned as Bill called his name, a frown on his face.

"Bill? You're in a hurry."

Bill slowed his steps as he handed over the papers he was holding. "Read these. There're about Jerry Lake. A real nice fellow he was not. Assault, fraud, extortion, attempted murder. Every single time he was charged, the charges were dropped. Same lawyer. Same judge. Same prosecuting attorney."

"I see a pattern here. Was he blackmailing them?"

"Lily's looking into it. I wonder how much he was being paid to go after Madigan."

"You're sure she's the target?"

Bill nodded. "The team recovered notebooks of his. She's named as a target. Silas wasn't at that time, but he may be now." Bill studied the last piece of paper he held. "I also found this. Silas has someone after him. I'm still trying to find out who and why."

"Silas? I find that hard to believe." Andrew reached for the paper, reading it carefully. "You'll need to talk to both of them, Bill."

"I'm heading that way now. Any word on Madigan's abductors?"

Andrew shook his head. "Nothing. It's like they vanished into thin air, but I know they didn't. They're watching them, I know it."

Silas stepped back from the door allowing Bill to enter. Bill had that look about him, Silas noted, that meant business.

"Bill. Come on through to the kitchen. Have you had your lunch?"

"Lunch? Is it that time already? No, actually I haven't. I don't want to put you to any trouble." He stopped as he saw Madigan turning from the stove. "Afternoon, Madigan."

"Bill. Come and sit. We have plenty." She slid a bowl of home-made soup and then a sandwich in front on him and then in front of Silas, stopping as he reached for a quick kiss.

Silas grinned at the blush on her face, then waited to pull her chair back for her.

"Bill. I think you're here for a reason, other than a free lunch." Silas grinned again at the frown on Madigan's face.

Bill laughed. "I am. This is good soup, Madigan. Beats canned soup any day."

"Thank you." She paused, her spoon in her bowl. "So, what do you have?"

Bill choked on the mouthful of soup. "Let's get right to it, shall we?"

She nodded. "It's taking up too much of my life and freedom. I want whoever it is stopped."

Bill wiped his mouth on his napkin, then laid his arms on the table, his eyes on Silas. "The body in the basement of the church was Jerry Lake. Andrew told you that. We have evidence he was paid to go after Madigan." At a noise from her, he looked at her, compassion in his gaze. "We don't know who yet. That's the thing. So you are still in danger. Silas, now you. We've been given evidence that someone is after you too. Who or why, we don't know. Whether it's related to Jerry Lake, we don't know that either. I need to know you two will take every precaution you can."

Silas and Madigan stared at one another, her face pale. He reached for her hand, clasping her cold one in his. "We'll take every precaution. But I think we have had someone hanging around the shrubs at the back, Bill. I've looked around. I don't see that anyone has been there. More a feeling I have."

"I'll take a look before I leave." He stood. "Thank you for the meal, Madigan.

And again, we need both of you to be very careful."

Silas walked back to the kitchen, pausing at the doorway as he watched Madigan just sitting, her chin propped on her hands, staring into space. He pulled his chair over and sat, wrapped her in his arms, his chin on her head.

"What are you thinking?" His voice was quiet.

"I'm thinking I need to find out who is it that's after us. Bill and Andrew are investigating but they don't seem to be getting too far."

"I see." Silas sat in silence for a while. "Then, that's what we'll do. We'll try and figure out who it is."

"But how, Silas? I have no idea how to start." She leaned back to study his face.

"I don't really either, but I know of someone who can help. It would mean a trip back to Riverville." He stood, reaching for her hands. "Let's get the kitchen cleaned up and then we'll head out. Hopefully Emma's around."

"Can't we do it from here?"

He stood, his eyes thoughtful. "We can, if that's what you prefer."

She nodded. "I would, Silas. I just don't feel safe traveling that distance. Not at the present."

He sighed, knowing she was right. A few minutes, and they were seated in the office, a call in to Emma at Tracker's. Disappointed not to reach her, Silas left a detailed message, asking for a call back.

"Now what, Silas?" Madigan dropped to the couch, her eyes staring at him. "What do you do on your days off?"

He laughed as he shrugged. "Take it easy. Visit friends. Read. Garden. What do you do on your days off?"

"About the same." She started to giggle. "We sound like a senior couple."

He laughed with her. "That we do. We do need to do some grocery shopping."

The two men followed them, watching for an opportunity to stop them, but none came. They walked through the stores after them, but didn't find the opportunity to force them to go with them. Frustrated, they followed them back home, parking down the street and watching as Silas drove into the garage and the garage door blocked their sight.

Chapter 13

A week later, Madigan walked away from the M&M Disaster Restoration office, heading for her car, then stopping as she remembered Silas had dropped her off that morning. She was content, she decided, even knowing that someone was after her. She really didn't miss the heavy work involved as part of the disaster response crew, but she missed the people on her crew.

She turned as she heard her name called, frowning for a moment, then her face clearing.

"Phoebe! How nice!" She leaned to hug Phoebe. "What are you doing here?"

"I've come to rescue you. Your Mom said you were done for the day. I'm off to the ladies' Bible study. Do you have time to come?"

Madigan chewed at her lip, then nodded. "Except Silas dropped me off this morning."

Phoebe started to laugh. "That's okay. We meet at our place. He'll come by and get you. In fact, we would like you both to stay for supper."

Madigan shrugged, looking down at her work clothes. "I'm not really dressed for a meeting."

"We have time. We can stop by your place and you can change. We really want you to come."

Madigan's eyes narrowed. "Who's we?"

"Silas' friends' ladies. I am sure he's talked about them all."

"He has." She stilled looked hesitant, then shrugged. "Why not?"

Silas came looking for her three hours later, stopping in Andrew's living room as he watched her laughing with Phoebe, before she looked up, her face lighting up as she saw him.

Andrew stood beside him, watching them before he glanced at Phoebe, getting her nod.

"Silas, you didn't tell me your friends and their wives had adventures like we're in the midst of!" Madigan's voice was full of laughter.

"Did I neglect to tell you that?" He sat beside her, drawing her close to him. "I'm sorry. I guess I just forgot. Did Phoebe tell you about their adventure?"

"She did. And I hear tell you suggested they marry so quickly." She smirked at him as Andrew and Phoebe laughed and Silas grinned.

The men watched Silas' house closely over the next few days, not seeing an opportunity to snatch either one of the couple. Their boss was getting frustrated. They couldn't understand why, as he had never said. Just told them to grab whichever one they could.

Silas watched from the window as the same car circled their block once again before reaching for his phone.

"Bill. Yes, the car's back. We've been seeing it a lot over the last few days. No, it's not one of the neighbour's. I can't get a glimpse of the plate but this is its description. Okay. Thanks." He turned as he felt Madigan's hand on his back.

"The same car again?"

Silas nodded. "Bill's sending in an unmarked patrol vehicle, to see if they can catch them. He wants us to stay inside for now."

"I'm tired of this, Silas. They're taking too much away from us."

"I know they are, but we can't let them win. They'll win if they catch us." He turned, walking back towards where she had gone to stand near the kitchen doorway and sweeping her into his arms. "I heard back from Emma."

"You did." Her voice was muffled against him. "What did she have to say?"

"Not a lot yet. She and Abe and their little one were away on vacation. She'll be working on it for us now. She did say she'd make it a priority." He sighed as he stepped back, his hands resting lightly on her shoulders. "I need to get to the church. What are your plans?"

She shrugged, her eyes on him. "I don't really know. I guess I've been so used to working, I never really thought what I'd do in my time off."

"I can drop you off at work, if you like. I'm sure your Mom would love your company."

She nodded. "Thanks, Silas. I would like that."

The men followed, Silas watching the car as he drove. He was worried, worried that they'd snatch Madigan again from her work, worried that she'd disappear and he'd lose the half of his heart he had just found.

Mary looked up as Madigan walked through the door. "Madigan! I didn't expect you today!" She reached to hug her daughter.

"I was bored, Silas had to go to the church, so here I am." She looked around. "What needs done today, Mom?"

"Actually, with you working in the office now, we've managed to get everything caught up. Filing is done. So we can to sit and have coffee." She watched her daughter's face. "What's wrong, Mads?"

"I'm worried about Silas, Mom. What if they take him on me?" Madigan wrapped her arms around herself, pacing the office area.

"Mads, what do we always do when we're this worried?" Madigan stopped at her mother's words, and her head dropped. Mary smiled. "Have you been praying?"

"I have, Mom, but sometimes it feels as if they're not going anywhere."

Mary drew her daughter down into a chair, then pulled one up for herself, reaching for Madigan's hands. She prayed, her prayer flowing through her daughter and bringing peace.

Madigan swiped at the tears on her face. "Thanks, Mom. I needed a Mom prayer."

Mary sat watching, a smile on her face, but questions in her heart. She hadn't liked that Madigan and Silas had married so quickly, without really getting to know one another. She wasn't aware of anyone else that she knew about that had done that.

Madigan bit her lip, then spoke. "Did you know Andrew and Phoebe married like we did, only knowing one another for less than a day? Silas suggested it. It was to protect Phoebe from her family."

Mary sat back, stunned. She knew the couple from church, not well. "You would never know that, Mads. How did you find out?"

"Phoebe. We're getting to be good friends. It was Andrew's suggestion that Silas and I marry. I'm glad he did, Mom. I can't imagine not having Silas in my life." She rose and turned away from her mother, walking towards the kitchen area. Her mother watched, not quite sure how to respond.

Silas looked up as Anna tapped at his partially opened door.

"I'm off, Silas. I'll lock up for you. The board members will be here in about thirty minutes."

Silas looked up, drawing his thoughts back from the study he was deep into, and glanced at the clock. He sighed. He knew it would be a stormy meeting and he wanted to spend time in prayer before it.

"Thanks, Anna, for all you've done today. You're off tomorrow, right? Then, we'll see you on Sunday."

Silas finally slid his folder from the table in one of the rooms, rising, his eyes on the other members of the board. He had known it would be a bad meeting and it had been. They had removed Dean from the board and he had not taken it well.

Silas walked out with Art, deep in conversation, not seeing Dean waiting for him. As he approached his car, Dean appeared, a fist drawn back. Silas did not have time to duck before he was down, his eyes closed, shouts rising from around him.

Art knelt beside Silas, his phone in his hand. He spun on his heel, his eyes on Dean as he was restrained and hearing the sirens approaching from the distance. Red and blue lights flickered over the scene as Dean was handcuffed and shoved into a patrol vehicle. Paramedics worked on Silas as he opened his eyes, sitting up and shaking his head, refusing to go to the hospital. He knew Madigan would be waiting up for him.

Art stood beside him as the last of the emergency vehicles left.

"I'm sorry, Silas. I never expected that."

Silas shook his head, regretting it. "I knew he wouldn't take it well. I just never expected violence from him."

Art sighed. "Now, we have to deal with him and the church. It's not getting any easier. He's been warned too many times."

Silas nodded, heading for his vehicle, his thoughts on Madigan. He knew she'd be worried. He quietly opened the house door, noting the low lights. He smiled. It was nice to come home to someone waiting, he thought. He searched the downstairs, stopping in his office and smiling once more as he saw the tray waiting for him. He turned, heading up the stairs, finding Madigan sound asleep. He turned, intent on going back down to the office, and then turned back. Not tonight, he thought. Tonight he just needed to fall asleep with his wife in his arms. He needed that comfort.

Chapter 14

*H*ands to her mouth, Madigan stared at her husband's face, aghast at the bruise that was now darkening. "Dean did that?"

He nodded, his eyes on her face. "He did. He was removed from the board and blamed me." He sighed as he reached for her. "They had to arrest him, Madi. That means an assault charge, but the responding officer said there were likely more charges that would be filed. Apparently they've been investigating him over the last few months."

She wrapped her arms around him. "And here I thought you'd be safe at the church." She leaned back. "Are you going in today?"

He shook his head. "No, I have home visits on the agenda. I would like you to come with me, if you would."

She stared at him and he saw the apprehension lurking in her eyes before they steadied and she nodded. "Just let me change to something more appropriate that jeans and a T-shirt and I'll go."

Hours later, as they walked away from the last house, Silas reached for her hand, noting her fatigue. "Thanks, sweetheart. I know how hard it was for you."

She tilted her head as she looked up at him. "It wasn't so bad, just a lot of questions." She started to laugh. "Mrs. Bradshaw was funny."

Silas joined her laughter, his thoughts on the petite ninety-year-old widow who had questioned them at length, then said a prayer of benediction over them. She was one of his people he liked to visit, loving her dry sense of humour and the wisdom she would impart.

"Now, off to dinner. Let's eat out tonight, Madi."

She nodded. "Ev's diner?"

He turned to her. "Unless you prefer somewhere else?"

She shook her head. "No, it's fine. I just have to get used to being under a microscope, that's all. I'm used to being in the background, not noticed."

"Never not noticed, Madigan." She looked up at him, surprised, her amber eyes questioning. "You've been noticed, sweetheart. You just didn't notice back."

She shook her head. "I guess I was so focused on work and family, I didn't notice." She looked up. "I'm so thankful you did. God has blessed us."

He tucked her into the vehicle, his eyes watching, frowning as he saw the truck waiting down the road. Sliding behind the wheel, he hesitated, knowing they would be driving a relatively deserted portion of the highway.

"Silas?" Madigan's soft voice reached his ear. "Is everything all right?"

He nodded, not wanting to worry her. "It is. Let's go eat. I know it's early but it was a late night last night, and I want to spend some time with my lady."

He watched as the truck pulled out and followed him, his heart in his throat. This was a fairly isolated section of town and he didn't want anything to happen to Madigan. He breathed a sigh of relief as he pulled into Ev's diner, watching as the truck pulled in too. He walked around to open Madigan's door, seeing the two men from the truck approaching him.

"Wait in the vehicle for a moment, Madi." He closed the door, leaning back on it, his eyes on the men before he relaxed.

"Joseph. Micah. How'd you track me down?"

Joseph grinned. "It wasn't hard. Mrs. Bradshaw called Leah. She said you were coming to visit her today and she was worried." He peeked past him at the window. "Leah told Abe and Abe sent us. Now, will you introduce us to your lady?"

Silas shook their hands, even as he laughed, reaching to open the door, pulling Madigan close to him. "Madigan, these are some good friends from Riverville. Joseph. Micah. This is Madigan."

She frowned as she looked at them before searching Silas' face. Her face cleared at the peace she saw there before she turned back to them. "Hi. Do you always follow people around?"

Joseph grinned as Micah nodded. "That we do, Madigan. That we do. We're security people. It's part of our job description."

Silas shook his head at Micah's comment, knowing full well their work was a lot more complex than that.

Silas slid into the booth beside Madigan, his arm draping around her as he pulled her close. Madigan listened to the quiet conversation between the men, realizing that they really were good friends.

She frowned as she watched the couple sitting across the diner from them, seated in such a way so as to keep an eye on them. Silas watched her face, then followed her eyes, a puzzled look on his face.

Joseph and Micah shared a quick glance, knowing something was up. Joseph excused himself for a moment, heading for the parking lot. Micah shared a look with Silas before nodding.

Joseph slid back into his seat, saying a quick thanks as Ev set their plates down. He looked up at Silas, shaking his head. Madigan watched the men, then the couple across from them. Something was going on but she wasn't quite sure what.

As they were heading back out to their vehicles, promises were made to get together with Joseph and Micah and their wives. With Madigan's attention on Joseph, Micah handed Silas a USB drive, with a quiet word that it was from Emma.

Madigan glared at her husband, brows lowered as he laughed at her. "It's not funny, Silas. You could have warned me better."

He reached to pull her to him, wrapping his arms around her. "I'm sorry. I really didn't know it was them. I never knew that Mrs. Bradshaw was Leah's great-aunt. She never ever said, either one of the ladies."

She shoved at him but he refused to let her go. "How many friends in security do you have?"

"Plenty. More than enough to keep you safe, if needed."

"You'd better be safe as well." She laid her head on his chest, listening to his heart beat. "Silas, what did Micah hand you?"

"You didn't miss that? A USB stick. From Emma. He said she found some interesting information for us."

She moved away from him, pulling at his hand. "Let's go take a look and see if there's something we need to pass on to Andrew and Bill."

Andrew looked up the next morning as he heard Silas' voice, rising with a frown on his face.

"Silas?"

"Andrew? You have a few minutes?" Silas held up the USB stick. "Emma sent some information I think you'll need to take a look at."

Andrew took it, all the while keeping his eyes on Silas. "You're bothered by what you found."

"I am. I never expected Emma to find what she did. I don't think any of us would have." He turned. "I'll leave it with you, Andrew. I have to be at the church shortly for a counselling session. Call me later."

Andrew watched Silas walk away, seeing the fatigue in his friend's body and demeanour. He sighed. He wanted this over for the couple. He knew how he had felt.

Bill appeared at his side. "Was that Silas?"

Andrew nodded, handing over the USB drive. "Check this out and follow up on anything we need to. Emma sent it over."

Bill stared at it and then at Andrew. "Seriously?"

Andrew nodded. "Silas asked her to check some stuff out for them."

Bill looked down at the USB drive. "Do you have any idea what's on this?" He looked up with a question on his face at Andrew's silence. "Andrew?"

Andrew shook his head. "I don't, but I know whatever is on it is weighing heavily on Silas."

Bill stood for a moment. "Knowing it's come from Emma, there's sure to be something on here we can use. I don't like it, Andrew. I have a bad feeling about this."

"I do too, Bill. Pray hard for those two. This is far from over and I just have a feeling it's going to very ugly before it's over." Andrew turned away, his thoughts already on the work awaiting him.

Bill stared down at the small piece of plastic in his hand, turning it over and over, praying as he had never prayed before. This would be explosive, he thought.

Silas walked his backyard, hands jammed into his jeans' pockets, his head bent as he thought through the last few days and weeks, his heart raised in prayer. He had no idea where or when it would end. He could see the stress in Madigan, could feel it in himself. He prayed that their faith would stay strong, that they would grow more together as a couple. He turned as he felt someone near him.

Madigan stood for a moment, her eyes on her husband, before she reached for him. They stood, arms wrapped around each other, as Silas prayed aloud for them. Both knew something big was about to happen and they needed to be prepared. Just what and when they had no idea.

Silas finally turned them towards the house. Tomorrow was Sunday again and he felt ill-prepared for it. Somehow he would make it through, he just knew God would do that. But his heart knew something was about to break loose and he didn't want his wife caught upon it.

Chapter 15

$\mathcal{S}$triding across the parking lot at the local conversation area, Silas searched for Madigan, finally finding her seated at a picnic table. He slid onto the seat beside her, reaching for her hand.

"You look troubled, sweetheart. And I don't think we should be out here." He searched the area, not really seeing anything.

She nodded. "I know we shouldn't. Silas, I'm tired of living like a prisoner. We need our freedom back. Did Andrew say anything about what you took him a week ago?"

Silas shook his head. "Nothing. I know they're following up on it. It's what they do. When they have something to share, they will."

She laid her head on his shoulder. "I know. I'm just impatient."

He sighed. "I am too. That's the thing of it. We have no idea how long this will be going on."

She sighed. "I want this over. Today. How do we go about doing that?"

"I'm not sure there's anything we can do." He turned as he heard a vehicle on the gravel parking lot. He rose. "Let's go, sweetheart. I don't like this."

He grabbed her hand and pulled her with him, heading for his vehicle. The vehicle cut in front of them, stopping them. Silas backed up as three men exited and approached him.

"Silas?" Madigan's voice was quiet.

"Madi, I need you to do something for me. Run! There's a forestry office about a mile up the trail. It's open. Head for it. Now!" He gave her a shove as he turned her to run. He turned to run after her, his foot slipping on the gravel and sending him down.

Two of the men were on him before he could rise, the third running after Madigan. She heard his shout to her to keep going and she sped up, running as fast as she could, hearing the pounding footsteps behind her. She glanced back, not seeing the man, but still hearing him. She ducked down a small nature trail and kept running, finally slowing to a stop and leaning against a tree. She had no idea how far she had run. She turned, not hearing anyone after her, then spun in a circle, realizing in her flight she had gotten lost. She turned in a circle once more, not sure where to go or how to get out of where she was.

The two men finally stood back from Silas, leaving him in a bloodied broken heap and turned to watch the third man approach. They spoke for a few minutes before one stood over Silas again, delivering a hard kick to his ribs, before they walked to their vehicle and drove away. The clouds finally let go of their heavy burden, the rain drops thudding the ground in an ever heavier manner, soaking Silas.

Five hours later, their friends were on a search for Silas and Madigan when they hadn't shown up for the couples' dinner, having no idea where to look for them. Two hours later, Sam pulled his vehicle into the parking lot, following a hunch. He stared at the car, running its plate, then shoving his door open, pulling his slicker tighter around him. It was dusk and the rain had finally ended, leaving just a fine drizzle. He walked towards the picnic area, his flashlight sending a broad beam around. His footsteps halted and then he ran forward, reaching for Silas, then for his radio.

"Dispatch, give me the chief! And I need units and paramedics as the east parking lot of the conservation area. Stat."

Andrew's heart sank as he spoke with Sam. "Just Silas? He's alive?"

"He is, Andrew. Not by much, but he's still alive. Whoever did this worked him over well. And I would say he's been lying here in the rain for hours." He stood back to let Ezra and Tom, the paramedics, work on Silas. He turned in a circle. "There's no sign of Mads. I have no idea if she was taken or if she ran." He walked towards the woods. "The rain's pretty much messed up any footprints I can see."

"All right, Sam. Thanks. I'll make the call to her family and then meet you at the hospital." Andrew paused. "Do you think there's a chance search and rescue could find her?"

"If she's in the woods, maybe. But we'll have to wait for morning now. I have a couple of officers here to watch. I'm heading over to the hospital with Silas."

Andrew pocketed his phone, his footsteps hurried as he looked for Bill.

"Bill, we have Silas. Sam found him. He's been beaten and left in the weather."

Bill spun from the copier he had been standing at, quickly gathering his papers and heading to dump them on his desk. "Madigan?"

Andrew shook his head as he pulled out his truck keys. "No word on her. She wasn't there. Sam can't tell if she was taken or if she ran. We're hoping to bring in search and rescue in the morning."

"I finally reached Silas' parents yesterday morning. Saul said they were heading home next week but would be on a plane today. It's a twenty hour flight for them."

Andrew and Bill ran for the Emergency Department doors, slowing to a walk as they entered. Members of the church milled around, while others sat, heads bowed in prayer for their pastor and his wife. Bill headed for the door to the examination rooms while Andrew searched for Madigan's people, his steps stopping as he recognized Emily and Saul Peters.

Saul stood as Andrew approached, his hand reaching out. "Thank you, Andrew, for finding him."

"I didn't expect you two back yet. Bill said you were leaving today." He reached to hug Emily.

"When our director heard what was going on, he sent us out on a private flight late yesterday afternoon, in time to connect with a late night flight to Oak City." He looked around, shellshocked and worried. "I have no idea what to do."

"Sit, my friend. It's your turn to be ministered to. I'm looking for Madigan's people."

"Madigan? Madigan Browne?" Emily and Saul exchanged a glance. "Why? Was she injured too?"

Andrew spun back to stare at them. "You really don't know?" When they shook their heads, Andrew sank into a chair near them. "Silas and Madigan have been married for about four weeks. It was really sudden."

Silas' parents stared at one another and then back at Andrew.

"We never knew. Silas can't reach us very well by phone and letters take so long to get to us." Emily reached for Saul's hand.

"Silas rescued her from danger, and then decided he loved her enough to marry her quickly to help protect her."

Saul nodded. "That would be Silas." He looked up as he saw Bill approaching.

Andrew rose and went to meet him. "We have a problem here, Bill. Silas' parents didn't know they were married."

Bill blew out a breath. "That's not good." He turned to look behind him. "The physicians are really worried about Silas, Andrew. He's been beaten badly. They're not sure how much he's injured internally. And then there's the exposure on top of that." Bill shot a look around, seeing Madigan's parents and brother just entering the hospital. "Her family's here now, Andrew."

Andrew turned, an unreadable look on his face. "I'll head back and see what they have to tell me about Silas. Can you get the two families together somewhere they'll have some quiet and won't be bothered by the press?"

Bill nodded. "I can. I know just the room. Sam said he was heading back out to the area. I wouldn't be surprised to see him head in there tonight."

Andrew paused. "I can see that. He needs to wait for morning. Let him know that. He can run the search but he needs to wait."

Fear driving her feet, Madigan kept running, away from the area, away from Silas, not knowing if he was alive or dead. She searched behind her as she paused to catch her breath, not seeing or hearing anything other than her ragged breathing. She pushed on through the rain, not finding the forestry building Silas told her to run to. Where was it? She had no idea how long she had been running for. She didn't realize it had been over a day and each step was taking her further and further away from help.

She paused again to swipe at the wet hair and sweat on her face, fatigue now weighing every step, every movement. She walked forward, suddenly finding the earth shifting under her feet, sending her to her back as the small landslide took her down the low hill. She screamed in fear, trying desperately to make it to the side, but not succeeding, feeling the rocks, roots and other sharp objects digging into her back. She lay still once the earth stopped moving, gathering her breath, gathering her strength to once more rise and go forward.

The pain almost stopped her dead in her tracks but she knew she had to keep moving. Where to, she had no idea.

Night and day became one for her as she struggled forward, pain and fever now her constant companions. She entered a clearing, hearing a stream, searching through bleary eyes to find it. She stumbled, her feet catching on an exposed root, sending her to the ground. Her head cushioned on her outstretched arm, her other arm curled around her face, she lay still. She no longer had the ability or strength to rise and move forward. Her eyes closed. Gradually the sounds of the woods came once more around her. Squirrels scurried by, stopping to inspect the strange object lying on the forest floor.

Hours later, quiet conversation disturbed the clearing, hushing the sounds of nature. The couple approached, then stopped before moving quickly towards the form on the ground.

The woman dropped to her knees, reaching for Madigan, a breath of relief coursing through her. "She's alive, Mike, but look at her back!"

Mike dropped to his knees beside his wife. "I know. How did she get here and how did she get so hurt? We're miles way from help." His gaze swept the area, trying to find her path.

Esther nodded. "I know. We're going to have to carry her out somehow, love, but it's too late tonight." She looked around. "I'll do what I can for her back but she'll need better treatment than what I can give."

An hour later, Esther had dressed Madigan's wounds as best she could, cleaning away dirt, mud and debris. Mike held Madigan as Esther managed to get some water down her, then laid her gently onto the sleeping bag. She reached for Madigan's ring finger, touching the engraved wedding band, thinking it looked so familiar.

"I wonder who she is?" Esther reached for Madigan's pockets, pulling out a phone and then her wallet. "She's Madigan Peters, Mike. Don't we know a Madigan Browne? It's such an unusual first name."

"We do. Her parents run the disaster restoration place." He reached for the wallet, flipping through it to try and find out more information, pausing as he came across a picture. "Esther. Look at this."

Esther moved over beside him, her hand going to his arm as she leaned in closer. "That's Silas." She looked over at Madigan. "Are they married? Emily never said anything." She reached for the wedding band again. "That's why this is so familiar. It was Mom's."

"Emily's too hard to get in touch with. And Silas may have tried to reach us but we've been travelling so much in the last while."

She nodded, her thoughts going to her nephew. "We have been." She stared at Madigan. "But that doesn't explain why she's out here, all on her own."

Mike closed the wallet, sticking it into his shirt pocket and buttoning the flap closed, his face thoughtful. "No, it doesn't. And I can guarantee you that if she's Silas', he won't stop until he finds her."

Early the next morning, Mike carefully gathered Madigan into his arms, wincing as she whimpered against the pain. He knew of no easy way to get her out of there. They were too far away for cell coverage and too far away from anywhere they could go to for help. Esther brushed the hair back from Madigan's face, then nodded as she headed out first. This was not how they had planned their trek through the area, but people came first, especially if they were family and it would appear that she was.

Hours later, they walked out into the conservation parking lot on the south side, heading for their vehicle. Mike waited as Esther opened the back door and then slid Madigan onto the back seat, Esther cradling her in her arms.

They didn't see the curious looks the patrol officer sent their way before he started his vehicle and followed them. Mike gathered Madigan up again in his arms and headed for the Emergency Room doors, surprise on the faces of the people in the waiting room as he headed for the clerk, who took one look and waved him through the doors.

Dr. John Knox looked up from his paperwork as the nurse approached.

"John? Someone just walked in with Madigan. She's hurt, really bad."

"Madigan? How?" He was on his feet heading for the exam rooms before she had totally finished her comment.

"I have no idea. The man said he and his wife were hiking and came across her."

He nodded. "Call Andrew or Bill. They'll need to know."

"Betty's doing that now."

John stood for a moment, his eyes assessing Madigan before he turned, surprise coming over his face.

"Mike? I didn't know it was you that found her."

"We did. Esther cleaned her back up as best she could, but it's bad."

"Her back?" John moved around the bed, reaching to roll Madigan to her side and then using a pair of scissors, slicing up the back of her T-shirt. He winced, then frowned at the cuts, scrapes and bruises. "What happened to her?"

"I would suggest a landslide of some kind. She was unconscious in the middle of a clearing when we found her late yesterday afternoon. We waited until this morning to walk out with her." Mike looked towards the door. "I need to find Esther and then we'll be going over to Silas' place."

John spoke absentmindedly, his thoughts already on treatment options for Madigan. "You carried her?" At Mike's nod, he turned back to his assessment. "Silas is upstairs in ICU."

Mike spun back around. "ICU? Why?"

"He was beaten severely. You didn't know?" John gave Mike a keen look. "Grab your wife and head up there. I think Saul and Emily are up there."

Mike and Esther stopped in their nephew's hospital doorway, their eyes on him, before an exclamation brought their eyes to the others in the room. Emily was across the floor and had her sister in her arms before Esther could react.

Saul looked up from where he stood, nodding at Mike, his eyes going to his wife and her sister, before he frowned.

"How did you two know to come here? We've been trying to reach you."

Mike walked forward. "We found Madigan out in the woods yesterday and brought her in today." He nodded towards Silas. "How is he?"

"Getting there." Saul looked at Emily, a puzzled look on his face. "What do you mean, you found Madigan?"

"She was out in the woods. We stumbled across her while we were hiking."

Andrew walked into the room at that point. "Mike. Esther. Thank you. I need to talk to you two to find out what you know. Can we do that now?"

They nodded, taking another look at Silas before following Andrew from the room.

Matthew and Mary stood at Madigan's bedside, worry etched on their faces as they listened to John explain their treatment options. Silas wouldn't be able to make the call so it would be up to them.

"Definitely surgery, John? There's no other way?" Matthew's voice was quiet as he spoke.

"Not really, Matthew. And we need to go now. The surgeon's prepping and they're here for her." He looked around at the noise from the hallway. "Head up to the surgical waiting room and they'll come find you."

Chapter 16

*S*ilas glared at his mother as she tried to prevent him from rising from the bed.

"You're not strong enough, Silas."

He shoved aside the blankets and reached for his robe to pull over his T-shirt and pajama pants and then shoved his feet into his slippers, hesitating for a moment to let his head clear. "She's my wife, Mom. I need to be with her. If you won't help me, then move aside."

Saul approached with a wheelchair. "Silas, here. I'll take you." His eyes met his wife's and she finally sighed and nodded. He wasn't their little boy any more, but a man grown and married. She did need to step back.

Silas waited for his father to step back before he wheeled his chair closer to Madigan's bed, his eyes tracing her face, watching as she lay on her side. He traced the IV lines running vital fluids and antibiotics to her veins, watched the monitors as they beeped and clicked. He finally pulled

159

himself as close as he could get, his hand reaching for hers before his other hand cupped her cheek. Tears tracked down his face as he remembered what he had been told. They hadn't been able to rouse her, John said, not even her mother's voice had gotten through. He had nodded, knowing he would be the only one who could reach her.

Andrew and Bill had been in to talk with him, letting him know they were no further ahead with the investigation. It had grown cold. Silas sighed, knowing that God would be the One who could and would move it forward. Soon, Lord, he prayed. Let this be over soon. This time, they almost killed us. I can't handle knowing I could lose Madi so soon.

She stirred, a sigh coming from her, as her eyes flickered. He waited, his heart in his mouth, as she finally opened her eyes, struggling to focus. Her hand reached for his and he clasped it close in his.

"Madi. Sweetheart. Come on. Look at me."

Madigan stilled, hearing her beloved's voice. Where was she? The last she remembered was being told to run. Her eyes finally focused on Silas.

"Silas?" Her voice cracked as she tried to speak through the dryness of her throat. "You're okay? But your face!"

"I know, sweetheart. They tried hard, but it didn't work."

"What didn't work?" She blinked even as she frowned.

"They didn't kill either one of us." He took a look at the door, then rising from the chair, he climbed onto the bed, cradling her carefully to him, mindful of the healing wounds on her back. "My aunt and uncle found you out in the woods and brought you back to me."

"Your aunt and uncle?" Her eyes slid shut. She didn't have the stamina or strength to stay awake any longer.

"Sleep, sweetheart. You're safe." Silas' head went down on hers and he slept as well, not seeing the nurse's surprise as she entered the room to check on Madigan's wounds and then her smile.

Saul looked up as the nurse exited and stood to go find his son, stopping as she shook her head.

"They're sleeping, Mr. Peters. Silas as well. We'll let them sleep for a while. They've been apart and through too much to tear them away from one another." She nodded at the door and he stopped there to watch, a smile crossing his face.

Andrew stood for a moment beside him, before he spoke. "I guess I don't get to talk to them now, do I?"

"Not right now, Andrew. Is there any news?"

"We're making progress, Saul, but it's not going great. I need to speak with all of the families and then with them. We're missing something, something that will break the case wide open. Madigan told Silas that she had had an incident when she was young that scared her thoroughly. None of her family knew about it. Silas is the only one she's spoken to and he didn't have a lot of information on it. I need to know more about that. Somehow it's linked to this. I'm just not sure how."

Saul nodded. "Why don't we meet down in the room they've set aside for us in a couple of hours? Maybe by then Silas will be awake."

Andrew took another look at his friend, his thoughts going back to what he and Phoebe had been through and how he had feared for his own wife's life at one point, before he turned and walked away.

Two hours later, Silas finally agreed, albeit very reluctantly, to meet with his family, Madigan's family and Andrew and Bill. He stared at the door, wanting to be out of there and back with Madigan. He had been told they were moving both of them to a room on a different floor, together, to make it easier for security to be put in place. His head jerked around as he felt his mother's hand on his arm.

"Silas. Andrew needs your attention."

Silas stared over at Andrew, catching the tiny shake of Andrew's head, and sighed. He knew at some point he would have to talk to his mother about her hovering.

"Silas, what has Madigan told you about what happened?" Andrew's voice cut through the chatter.

"About what happened when she was 10?" At Andrew's nod, he shrugged. "Just that she was locked up somewhere it was totally black, that she couldn't get out, that finally someone let her out, gave her something to drink and sent her home. She's been absolutely terrified of the dark since then." He heard an exclamation from her parents and turned. "She said she had never told anyone until she told me. She said she couldn't. That whoever had done it to her threatened her family. I asked and she couldn't remember exactly what the threat was. She's buried it too deep now to remember, and I won't put her through anything to try and bring it out." He stared at her father until Matthew nodded.

"Did she say who?"

Silas stared at his hands, knowing he would have to say and not wanting to. He finally raised his head, his eyes on Mitchell. "Jerry Lake."

Quick words broke out at that between Madigan's family and his parents. His aunt and uncle sat back, not knowing who that was. Silas looked up as he heard rubber-soled shoes heading their way and then stood and walked towards the surgeon where he stood waiting.

"Darrell?"

"Silas. How are you? You've been in our prayers, my friend." Darrell Abbott looked past him, then motioned for Silas to follow him. "I need to talk to you about Madigan."

Silas' face blanched. "Not more surgery, please. Don't tell me that."

Darrell smiled as he shook his head. "No, actually, no more surgery. She's recovering much better than I had even prayed for. But I did need to talk to you about what we're facing." He pointed at a chair in the lounge. "Sit for a moment." Darrell sank into a chair beside Silas. "It's so good to be able to get off my feet. It's been a busy few days."

Silas nodded, his heart in prayer for his friend. "I hear you. You've been on call now for how many days? Three or four?"

"Three. This ends the on call for a week or two." He slid his eyes closed, resting for a moment, knowing Silas would grant him that much. "Now. About Madigan."

"Yes?"

"I'm having the plastic surgeon take a look at her back tomorrow, but I don't expect he'll need to do anything. If all goes well, I expect we'll be releasing you both the next day. A home care nurse will come in to change Madigan's dressing for you." He watched Silas absorb his words. "Do you have any questions?"

Silas snorted. "Just who did this. Andrew's at a loss and so I am. I have no idea."

"Dean?"

Silas shrugged. "It may be, but this doesn't feel like him. I can't figure it out. I don't have any enemies, and I can't see Madigan having any, unless she's seen something on one of her jobs that she shouldn't have." Silas's voice died away as he said that.

Darrell looked at him. "I think you've just solved it, Silas." He looked towards Andrew who stood in the doorway. "Has Andrew looked into any of those?"

Silas looked up, catching the look on Andrew's face. "I have no idea. Have you, Andrew?"

"Never really thought about that, Silas, but I think you and Darrell are correct. I'll need to sit down with Matthew and see what she's been working on in the last few years and what they worked on around the time she was ten. It may go back that far, and from what you said, I think it does."

Andrew sat for a moment, his eyes on Silas, before he spoke. "Silas, what can we do for you?"

Silas looked up, surprised. "What do you mean?"

"I mean, you're there for us, each one of us, every time we need you. You never ask for help, for anything for yourself. What do you need?"

"For this to be over, so that Madi and I can get on with our lives." He blinked back tears. "I almost lost her, Andrew. Whoever this is almost took her from me."

"And you from her." Andrew searched the corridor, seeking an answer. "I'll sit with Matthew and Mary and go through their jobs. I know they've been in to crime scenes. We'll start there first and work out to other disasters. There's an answer there, Silas. I know there is."

Silas stood, his heart heavy. "Find it before something more happens. That's all I ask." His steps were weighted as he walked away from his friend.

Silas' arm around Madi was the only thing that kept her from falling back down the stairs as he helped her to their room at home. She sank onto the bed, leaning into him as he sat beside her.

"Do you want to shower or just lie down?"

"I would love to shower but I think I'll lie down for now. Come ask me again in a couple of hours." She reached to kiss him. "Thank you, Silas. I love you so much."

He wrapped his arms around her, his cheek on her head. "I love you too, sweetheart. Now, let's get you lying down and I'll be back in a while. Do you want anything?"

She shook her head. "Not right now. Thank you." Her eyes were closed and she was asleep before he had covered her with a light blanket.

He stood, anger growing within him, anger he knew he had to let go of, but it still grew. Lord, why? Why Madi?

He turned, pulling the door partly closed behind him before he headed to one of the spare rooms and stood, staring out into the backyard, not seeing anything. He could hear faint conversation from downstairs and then the opening and closing of the front door. He sighed, knowing he would have to talk to his mother and not quite sure if he could express himself in such a way that she didn't take offence at what he needed to say.

He looked in surprise as he saw only his father waiting in the kitchen, a cup of coffee in front of him, and a sandwich and coffee at Silas' place.

"Where's Mom?"

Saul looked up at the words. "I sent her home. You don't need her hovering over the two of you. I just waited to make sure you were settled, then I'm heading home." He pointed to Silas' chair. "Sit. Eat. I'll talk to her, son. She's afraid and with her, fear does this. She'll hover."

"She does and we really don't need that. I get where she's coming from but Madi and I - we'll take care of each other."

"I know you will, son. Just realize that your Mom missed out on stuff with you and it will take time for her to get over that." Saul's hand came down on his son's arm. "For me too. I'm glad you have Madigan, but I wish we could have been here for you."

"Thanks, Dad." Silas sat back. "Do you get a sense of where the investigation is going or anyone that we need to pass names on for?"

Saul shook his head. "Not really, Silas. I think Andrew and Bill are doing their best that way."

ʃtaring down at the documents laid out on the table in the conference room, Andrew rubbed his neck. This is what he had been looking for, and it had been there all along. They had missed it. He looked up as he heard footsteps approaching, Bill hesitating as he saw Andrew's look.

"What did you find, Andrew?"

"This!" He beckoned Bill over, pointing at pictures and property documents. "Somehow, we missed this. This is who it is."

Bill drew in a sharp breath. "That's not good. How'd we miss it?"

Andrew shrugged. "It got buried in the pile for one thing. Another thing is that Matthew was able to track back to some work they did around the time Madigan was ten and found the names for us." He looked around. "We have to find these men, Bill. They're hunting for Madigan. I fear for her life if they find her."

"Are you heading out to talk to Silas and Madigan?" Bill picked up the next pile and his hand froze. "Andrew? Did you see the names on this one?"

Andrew shook his head and peered over Bill's shoulder. "Oh, I don't like that. Not one bit."

"He's out to get Silas, now that Dean's off the board. He blames him. He's been pretty vocal about it. Most people think he's harmless, but I don't think he is."

Andrew agreed. "Let's see where we go with this in the next day, and then I'll make a point of talking with Silas and Madigan. Right now, Silas says they're trying to stay quiet. He's worried about Madigan doing too much."

"He's right to worry. She'll be back at work or involved in the church more than she should be before she's really ready to." Bill looked up as an officer approached. "Yes, Walter?"

"Silas is here to see one of you. He said it didn't much matter which one."

Bill and Andrew shared a look as they both turned to follow Walter to the front of the building. Silas stood there, a small metal box in his hands, his eyes watching his friends walk towards him.

"Come on back, Silas." Andrew pointed to his office. "And what do you have there?"

"I really don't know, Andrew. It showed up on my doorstep this morning. I haven't opened it yet. I thought I'd leave it for you two."

Bill reached for his phone, calling in a crime scene tech. "How be we go into the conference room instead of your office, Andrew?"

"You take that and meet the tech. Call me when it's cleared." He turned to Silas as Silas sank into a chair. "How are you feeling?"

"Tired and sore. Worried." The shadows were getting deeper in Silas' eyes as the circles darkened under them. "I need to protect Madi and I don't know how."

"I know that feeling, my friend." Andrew sat back in his chair, his eyes on his friend. "We've made some progress. Whether you like it or not, Dean's family is involved and have been since the beginning."

Silas slowly nodded. "That's what I thought. There have been two groups, haven't there?"

"Why would you ask that?"

"Too much difference in the style of attack." Silas finally looked up and at Andrew. "I want to send Madi away somewhere but I know that won't help. They'll only follow her, won't they?"

"More than likely. Listen, both Richard and Don have said they're available."

Silas shook his head. "Thanks, but I don't think so. It would be putting more people at risk."

"It's what they do, Silas. Abe's volunteered as well."

Silas drew a deep breath and then stood. "Thank them for me, Andrew. If it comes to it, I'll send Madi away with them."

"She won't go without you."

Silas nodded. "I know, but she may have to." He turned to leave. "Thanks once more, Andrew. If it comes down to it, I'll resign as pastor and take Madi somewhere else." With that, he walked away, leaving

Andrew standing in his doorway, staring after him.

And he would do that, wouldn't he, Lord, to keep his people safe? Let us solve this before it gets to that point.

He looked up as Bill approached, Bill looking around for Silas.

"Silas has gone?"

"He did. He didn't wait around. I suspect he's either heading home or to the church. Do you need to talk with him?"

Bill nodded. "We do. This is what we found in the box." Bill handed over the evidence bag with the photos and letter in it.

Andrew studied the pictures and the read the note. "They're not playing around, are they? We need Richard or Don in on this. Silas has said no. I'm not giving him an option at this point. It's either one of them or we stick them away somewhere."

"And I think he'll take her and run before we can do that." Bill was frustrated. "How do we keep them safe? I have officers out now searching for Dean and his sons and for the brothers of Jerry Lake. Not much luck right at the moment. They've gone underground."

Andrew nodded, a thoughtful look on his face. "Try finding Old Dougie. He might have a lead as to where they are."

"I'll look for him, but he's missing too."

"When was he last seen?"

"A week ago? Maybe less."

Silas turned as Madigan walked towards him through the sanctuary. She had tracked him down that Friday afternoon. He reached to hug her, cradling her close to him.

"Miss me?" He laughed as she poked him.

"Always." She looked around. "What were you up to this afternoon?"

"I have that wedding tomorrow, just a small private one, and I wanted to make sure everything was in order. You are coming, aren't you?"

She looked up at him, surprised. "I wasn't asked, was I?"

He nodded. "They specifically asked for you to be here. It's the first wedding I'll be officiating since we married. It's all part and parcel of being my wife."

She nodded. "Then I guess I will be. Is this what a pastor's wife has to look forward to?"

He laughed as he turned her towards his office. "Part of the job, sweetheart. You'll do fine. You're interested in people and can get them to talk to you so easily. That's a big step right there. There are things I can't share, and the same will go for you. We have to respect their privacy and trust. But if something really bothers you, ask if you can share with me. Most times they'll agree."

"Did Andrew say anything about that box?"

Silas shook his head. "I left before Bill came back about it. Andrew wants to bring in one of the security teams to be with us until this is resolved. I told him I'd take you far away first."

Madigan perched on the corner of Silas' desk, her toes idly rocking his chair as he sat watching her. "Don't rule it out. It may be an option that we have to consider. We've had to do in on job sites, bring in security just because of the danger and the threats." She looked up at him as he made a sound. "You didn't realize that it was so dangerous?" She reached for his hand. "It has been. That's part of why Dad's glad I'm no longer out there on the crew. We have some women, but they're a lot tougher than I am." She watched Silas digest what she had said. "So, like I say, we may need to consider it. I pray we don't. Who would you choose?"

"Between Don and Richard? Either one, but Don is from this town. Actually, he goes to church here as does his team. Have you ever met them?"

She frowned. "I'm not sure that I have. You'll have to introduce me on Sunday, if they're here."

"I will do that. Now, I have a couple of hours of work to do. What would you like to do?"

She held up a book. "I came prepared. If it's okay with you, I'll just curl up in a chair and read until you're ready to go. If you need me to step outside while you take or make a call, I can do that."

Andrew stood for a moment at Silas' open office door, watching the two, before he knocked. Bill stood beside him.

Silas looked up, his heart sinking as he saw them standing there before he waved them in. "I'm not liking that both of you are here."

Andrew shook his head. "We're not liking it much, either. Madigan. How are you feeling now?"

She took her time in replying, first searching their faces, then that of her husband. "I'm not sure how I should be feeling right about now. Somehow, I don't think you've come to tell us you've solved everything."

Andrew sighed. "I wish I could. But I have news. We've found Jerry Lake's family. He was the last. They're all buried up in Oak City. So that doesn't help us out much."

"No, it doesn't. But why us?" Silas watched Madigan, noting her discomfort.

"I don't think we'll ever know. He didn't leave anything behind that would tell us that." Andrew turned as he heard a choked sound from Madigan.

She was staring at the floor. "Try Bobby Whyte. They were always close friends. He may have been the one who helped him lock me up. I know he didn't do it alone."

"You never mentioned that, Madigan." Andrew shared a look with Bill.

"That's because I buried it so deep, I never wanted to think about it again. Now, it's all coming to the surface. Try Bobby, Russell Whyte, their cousins. Sam knows who they all are. He was one of the ones who helped protect us girls from that gang when we were in elementary school." She finally looked up, her eyes finding Silas. "I'm sorry, Silas." Tears pooled in her amber eyes.

He was beside her in an instant, his arms reaching for her. "Ssh. It's okay. We know that's what happened." He looked up. "Anything else?"

Bill spoke. "The ones who beat you so badly, Silas? We now have names and have put out arrest warrants, but they've fled town for now. The surrounding departments are on the look out for them. But somehow I don't think they're finished with you. Not quite yet."

"Well, isn't that comforting?" He looked down at Madigan, then back up. "Anything else?"

"I just wish you'd reconsider having someone with you."

Madigan peeked around from where she was hidden in Silas' arms. "We've talked about that and both agree that Don would be our first choice, but only if it becomes absolutely necessary."

Andrew and Bill shared another look. They hadn't expected that response.

"What changed your mind?" Andrew was curious.

"Silas doesn't realize that Dad's work can sometimes very dangerous and that we've had to bring in security on job sites. So it would be no big deal for me. For him, yes, as he's never had it before."

Andrew nodded. "Then, I'll talk to him. You are going to need it, if the scuttlebutt we're hearing is correct."

With that, the two officers left, leaving the young couple staring after them.

"I thought he'd give you a harder time, Silas."

"To tell you the truth, so did I." Silas reached for her hand, after tidying away his paperwork. "Let's go home. It sounds as if we'll be having company around us for a while. I don't like it."

"Neither do I. But if it keeps us safe, so be it."

Silas didn't like that, but he realized they may have no choice. He vaguely recognized the names Madigan had mentioned but not well enough to know who they were.

"Do you have any photos of those men?" He asked as he tucked her into his car.

She looked up, a thoughtful look on her face. "I should do, in my yearbooks. They're still at Mom's. Let's stop and grab them. Maybe you can identify someone."

Chapter 18

Silas stood back from their front door later that night. Don, one of the security team leaders, stood there, his hand outstretched to shake Silas'.

"Don. That was quick. Andrew called you?"

Don shook his head. "No, actually it was your wife. Madigan, is it?"

Silas stared at him. "Madi did? She never said a word."

Don grinned. "That's what she said, that she hadn't told you but that the two of you had talked about bringing me in."

Silas stood watching Madigan for a moment before he spoke, startling her as she worked in the kitchen.

"Madigan, Don's here."

She spun, hand to her throat. "He is? Oh, good. Hi. I'm Madigan."

"And I'm Don." He shook Madigan's hand and then slid into a chair at the table

Silas pointed to. "Now, what can I do for you?"

Silas set cups of coffee down in front of them and then frowned at the pad of paper and pen Don had laid on the table. "You came prepared, I see?"

Don laughed. "I did. You should know that by now, Silas." He studied the young couple, around his own age he thought. Silas he highly respected as his pastor and it troubled him the problems they were facing.

"Where do we start? With the body in the church basement?" Don looked up at that. "You hadn't heard about that? Madi found a body in the basement when she went to lay hose, is that how you say it, Madi? We were run down that afternoon. Since then, things have just snowballed."

"I have talked to Andrew, and he has indicated what all you are going through. Now what? What do you want from us?"

Madigan spoke up. "I'm not really sure, Don. I think I just wanted to talk to you, to get your feel on what we should be doing. Silas can't leave his people. I don't want him to do that."

Don nodded, then spoke at length, bringing up various scenarios they could face and what they could do to protect themselves. He finally rose, tucking his pen back into his pocket. "Go over everything. Make your decision. And then call me."

Silas walked him back to the door. "Madi's not sure about any of this, you know."

"Neither are you." Don stood for a moment, his eyes scanning the area, feeling danger approaching, but not seeing anything. "It's coming back at you hard, Silas. Let us help."

"I'll call you. Thanks for stopping by."

Silas stood for a moment after Don had driven away, not quite sure how to approach his wife. He felt her hand on his back and reached to draw her down onto the love seat on the front porch.

"Thanks, sweetheart."

"For what?"

"For calling Don. For finding out what our options are." He snuggled her close to him. "I really don't know which way to go."

She shook her head. "Neither do I. But you have a big day tomorrow, love."

He rose, his hand extended. "We both do."

❀ ❀ ❀ ❀

A week later, Silas and Madigan headed into the church, planning on meeting three other couples there for a planning session. Andrew and Phoebe were one of the couples as well as their friends Adam and Candace and Samuel and Aideen. Small talk consumed the first few minutes, and then the ladies separated from the men. Neither group heard the doors open and quiet footsteps sounding. Six men in black, masks in place, walked quietly through the building, separating into the groups, one to follow the ladies, the other the men.

Silence met the group of men as they entered the room where the ladies were seated. Madigan's breath drew in sharply. This is it, she thought. They've come for us. Lord, protect us. Get us out of here alive and in one piece.

The ladies remained still, hardly daring to breathe as the two men stood, their eyes on the ladies.

Silas looked up as he heard the door close, his pen falling to the floor as he saw the four men enter. He heard a sound from Andrew and knew this was it. Lord, now what? We're even in numbers but they have the weapons. What about our ladies, Lord? Protect them.

The four friends stood, watching, waiting, not sure what to expect. The men just stood watching them, not saying a word. Andrew's hand was in his pocket and he tried hard to find the buttons to push to call for help. One of the men finally spoke.

"Phones. On the floor." When the men didn't move, the man stalked towards them, his weapon raised. "Now!" He watched as the phones were dropped to the floor, his eyes narrowing as he saw the light on Andrew's phone. "Who did you call?"

Andrew stared back, not saying a word, watching as the weapon was raised higher and pointed at him. A sudden commotion in the hall had the man turning and walking away, out into the hall. Ten minutes later, he returned, speaking quietly to the other three men. They turned to the four friends, eyes narrowed.

Samuel and Jonah were shoved to the floor, bound and then gagged. Silas and Andrew were shoved from the room and the door shut behind them. Samuel and Jonah struggled with their bonds, unable to loosen them, frantic to get free and find their wives.

Andrew and Silas were shoved roughly from the church towards a van. They could see Phoebe and Madigan being forced into a second van. They couldn't see the other two women and exchanged worried glances. Shoved down on the floor, the two men prayed as they had not prayed before. They had no idea where they were heading, who had them, or if their wives would be in the same place as they would end up.

Hours later, a patrol vehicle stopped in the church parking lot, surprised to see vehicles still there. The officer knew that there were few meetings on a Tuesday night, and if there had been a meeting, it would be over with by now. He reached for his radio, asking for backup, then, weapon drawn, headed for the church, searching through the rooms, stopping in surprise as he found the two women, bound to chairs. He quickly released them, listening to their words before he motioned them to come with him. He headed for the room down the hall and found Samuel and Jonah, quickly releasing them as well.

Bill stood, his eyes stern, face neutral as he listened to his friends. His heart sank even as he prayed. "How long, Samuel?"

"Four hours? Something like that?"

Jonah nodded. "We were here just before six and it was only about fifteen minutes later we were ambushed and the ladies separated from us. They took Andrew and Silas out without saying much of anything."

Bill shook his head. "They just walked them out?" When the men nodded, he sighed. "And you were left here. You didn't notice any odd about them?"

Jonah shook his head. "Nothing. Dressed all in black, masks on. Only one spoke and that was to ask our phones be dropped to the floor and then who Andrew had tried to call."

Bill picked up Andrew's phone. It was locked. "I would suspect he was trying to call for help, but didn't get the call completed." He turned to the ladies. "Nothing to add?"

They shook their heads, standing with their husband's arms around them.

Bill nodded. "Okay, we'll get your statements and then you'll be able to go. If you think of anything, anything at all, call me or Lily."

He turned, heading for the parking lot, knowing he would see little in the dark, but still determined to try. Lily approached him, worry on her face.

"Bill?"

"Yeah?" Bill stopped for a moment, drawing his hands down his face. "Whoever it was took Andrew and Phoebe and Silas and Madigan."

"Oh, no! Who was the real target?"

Bill spun at her words. "What did you just say?"

She stared at him, taking a step back at his words and the force of them. "I just wondered who the real target it? Which one of the couples?"

"I would say Silas, but it doesn't make sense to take Andrew, unless he knows something and doesn't realize it." Bill pulled Lily with him. "Come on. We're going to go back through that pile Andrew gave us this morning. There has to be something there."

Andrew laid his head back against the bare wall. He and Silas had been roughly thrown into the room and the door locked behind them. They had both searched for an exit, even a crack in the door they could work on, and found nothing. Their eyes met, their thoughts alike, praying for their wives.

Hours seemed to pass. Silas dozed, not meaning to, but fatigue caught up with him. Andrew would rise and pace every hour or so, trying to get a feel of where they were and who had taken them.

Phoebe turned from the window, having tried in vain to raise it once more. "We can't get out of here, Madigan. What are we to do?"

Madigan was slumped against the door, her eyes shadowed. "I have no idea, Phoebe. I wonder where Silas and Andrew are. Did you see them at all?"

Phoebe shook her head. "Not at all. Though there was a second vehicle that followed us. Maybe they were in that." She paced, her arms wrapped around herself. "Why, Madigan? Why did they take us and not the other ladies? If they took us, did they bring our guys as well?"

Madigan rose to her feet, stretching, then moving towards Phoebe. "I would suspect they did and that they'll use us again each other."

Phoebe nodded. "I agree. I just don't get why."

"Neither do I. Andrew must have a clue. He said he was getting close to finding out who." Madigan spun, and then leaned back on the door, her stance defiant. "Don was by and offered some suggestions." She looked down, her heart hardening. "We didn't get a chance to try any of them."

Phoebe had been watching her face. "Don't harden your heart, Mads. God is here. He will protect us and get us out of this."

Madigan snorted. "Like He always does. Why doesn't He stop it in the first place?"

"I have no idea. I've told you what I went through before Andrew rescued me and what we went through as a couple." She reached for Madigan's hand. "Come on. Let's try and figure this out. Who do you suspect?"

Madigan's eyes studied her friend, barely visible in the moonlight streaming through the window. "I have an idea but I can't prove it. Andrew thinks there are two parties. I don't. I think it's only one and he's from the church."

Phoebe stared at her for a moment and then nodded. "I think you're right. It would come from inside the church with Silas, now wouldn't it? I'm sure Andrew and Bill and

Lily have all been searching that out, but let's you and I think it through."

For the next couple of hours, the two women talked back and forth, bringing up one name after another and rejecting most of them, finally settling on one no one would suspect.

"I think we have it, Phoebe. Just how do we prove it when we're here?" Madigan reached for her pocket and pulled out a phone.

"Mads? You have a phone?"

She nodded. "I do. I'll only get one chance with it, so who do we send a message to?"

"Bill. Let him know who we suspect and why. Then turn it off and hide it somewhere they won't find it." Phoebe shook her head. "I have no idea how you managed to hide that."

"After what happened, I found a small pay-as-you-go phone that would hide in a pocket. Now to remember Bill's number. There we go. The text has gone." She heard footsteps in the hallway even as the dawn was breaking. She searched quickly, finding a small crack just big enough to hide the phone in. She didn't get it turned off, deciding to leave it on, hoping Bill could track it.

The door slammed open, and their captor stood there, his hard gray eyes searching their faces, before he reached for their arms and shoved them through the doorway ahead of him. They exchanged startled, frightened glances, not quite sure what was up.

Shoved into a room, their eyes searched for their husbands, finding Silas and Andrew standing against the far wall, weapons held on them. Their eyes met, each assuring the other they were fine. Andrew's eyes flickered from Phoebe to Madigan, a small frown appearing, sensing they had been up to something. What did they do, he wondered? Lord, if it gets us out of here, I'm all for it.

Andrew was pushed roughly forward and out the door, fighting to get back to Phoebe. His captor raised his weapon and Andrew slumped to the dirty, dusty floor, blood trickling down his temple from the blow from the gun barrel. Phoebe cried out and tried to get to Andrew but was restrained. Madigan stood in shock, her eyes on Andrew before a small sound from Silas had her turning back towards him. He was shoved up against the wall, a forearm tight against his throat, the barrel of a gun pointed under his chin. He had frozen in place, his tortured eyes on Madigan as she was pulled from the room. His assailant waited, then backed from the room, his weapon pointed directly at Phoebe. Silas had taken a step forward, then stopped, knowing if he made another move, Phoebe would be the one to pay for it.

Andrew's hands were bound behind his back before he was hauled to his feet and shoved from the building, his feet stumbling over each other as he tried to get his balance back, his head pounding from pain. Madigan twisted and turned, trying to break free, but not succeeding as the grip on her arm tightened. Blindfolds were slapped across their eyes and Madigan's hands were bound as well. Slumped in a van seat, Madigan's heart broke. Would she ever see Silas again? Would Andrew and Phoebe ever be together again? Lord, why? Why did You allow this? I thought You'd protect us, free us. Instead, we have been separated and who knows what will happen now. Dear Lord, I don't have faith anymore to believe. I just can't do it. Broken, Madigan could feel the tears prickling at her eyelids and then trickling down her face.

Chapter 19

*S*ilas slumped to the floor, his head buried on the arms he had folded on his upraised knees. Madigan was gone and he had no confidence that he would ever see her again. He could hear Phoebe's soft steps as she paced, knowing her heart was breaking as well now that Andrew was gone. He raised his head, determination taking the place of despair. He rose, his eyes on the door. He couldn't remember if he had heard it lock or not.

Phoebe's hand on his arm stopped his forward motion, and he stopped, his head turning to watch her face, the track of her tears tracing through the dirt. He frowned, not quite sure of what he was seeing on her face.

"Madigan had a phone." Phoebe's voice was barely audible. "She was able to get a message out to Bill."

Silas stared at her. "A phone? How?"

She shook her head. "I have no idea. If we can get back to that room, I know where she hid it."

"I don't think they locked the door." Silas moved forward once more, his feet as silent as he could make them, reaching for the knob and twisting it. The door cracked open and he froze, not knowing if someone was on the other side. He searched the room but found nothing he could use as a weapon.

Phoebe followed on his heels as he walked out the door, looking for their abductors and seeing no one. He searched the rooms on the second floor, and then ones on the first floor. Phoebe walked across the room they had been held in and reached for the phone, finding it still on but with little charge left. She quickly sent a text to Bill, asking for help, letting him know that Andrew and Madigan were no longer with them.

"Now what, Silas?" She pocketed the phone as she followed him out the door into the open, her eyes staring in shock as to where they were. "We're still in town? They drove us around for so long."

"They did. That was to confuse us, I would think." He spun in a circle, not seeing anyone. "I don't see them, Phoebe. Where are they?"

"I don't know, Silas. I'm scared." Her eyes were shadowed as stress showed on her face. "I know God has them in His hands, but I want Andrew here, now, with me."

"I know, Phoebe." His head turned as he heard a vehicle. "Come on. Into the woods. Let's not get caught again."

They ran, dust kicking up under their feet. Silas slid to a stop, his arm up to shove Phoebe further into the woods if needed. Then, he relaxed.

"It's Bill and Sam." He walked out of the woods.

Bill spun as he heard his name called and ran towards them. "You two are okay? What happened? Where are Andrew and Madigan?"

Silas shook his head. "We're fine. Whoever it was took Madigan and Andrew with them. Andrew was hurt, how bad I'm not sure."

"Phoebe?" Bill's attention turned to her. "Did they hurt you?"

She shook her head. "Not physically, but mentally, emotionally, they're messing with us."

Bill turned as Sam approached, shaking his head. He sighed. No evidence, just these two. "Let's get you back to the department and get your statements. Phoebe, you and I need to have a talk about that text message."

"Text message? The one we just sent? Why?" Silas stared between the two, a puzzled look on his face. He had forgotten Phoebe's comment about the message Madigan had sent.

"Not that one, Silas. Madigan got one out this morning, naming someone in the church both she and Phoebe suspect as being the ringleader in this."

Silas' steps stopped as he stared first at Bill and then Phoebe. "In the church? Phoebe?"

She shrugged. "We had time to talk. Madigan has an insight into people I've never seen before. She picks up on something about them. She said this particular person is one she has never felt comfortable around, even when you two married. There was something evil that she picked up on."

Silas nodded. "She does do that. Who is it?"

Bill and Phoebe shared a look and Bill gave a short nod. The shocked look on Silas' face when Phoebe spoke the name alerted them to the fact that Silas had never ever considered him.

"Are you serious? Him?" At Phoebe's nod, he ran his hands through his hair. "Wow! I have no idea what to say!"

Bill closed the car door after them, then stood, eyeing the area. The crime scene team had arrived and was searching, but he doubted they would find much evidence. He raised his eyes, feeling watched.

The watcher stared. How did the police get there that quick? He hadn't had a chance to make the call yet, but here they were. Who in their group had contacted them? He slipped away, rushing to find their leader and let him know what was up.

The leader turned as he heard the words, anger building in him. He stalked to the room Andrew and Madigan were tied up and stood, his eyes glittering through the eye holes in the mask he had pulled back on. He searched their faces, what he could see below the blindfolds. Anger continued to build. Someone had alerted the police and he intended to find out who. He stormed from the room, intent on questioning all his men and women.

"Who called the police?" His angry eyes bored into each one, not accepting that no one had jumped in too soon.

"None of us did. We were all together and not one of us used our phones."

"Did you search them?"

"We took their phones from them before we took them from the church." The spokesman for the group looked around and saw the nods from each one. "I have no idea how the police knew."

The leader spun, his eyes on the door to the room, knowing his people spoke the truth as they saw it but somehow someone had led the police directly to the two. Now, he would have to do some huge coverup.

"Keep an eye on them. I'll be back tonight and we'll have answers then. Call me if anything comes up, and I mean anything. We've gone too far to fail now."

The group nodded, then three of them walked out after the leader, leaving three to watch. One of them headed into where Andrew and Madigan were, taking them food and water.

Madigan refused to eat, not knowing if it had been drugged. Andrew took the water, knowing he needed to stay hydrated. They were bound once more after a few minutes. Andrew cocked his head as he heard the door shut and the lock click closed.

"Madigan?" His voice was soft.

"What?" Madigan's voice was angry before she sighed. "I'm sorry, Andrew. It's not your fault."

"And it's not yours. Are you okay?"

"I am. How's your head? They hit you really hard."

He sighed, twisting his neck to try and relieve the pain. "It hurts. I've had worse but I have nothing I can take for it. I'll be okay." He listened. "Did you recognize any of the voices?" When she didn't reply, he turned his head as if he could see her. "Madigan?"

"Yeah, I did. And you won't like who it is."

"Who, Madigan?"

"Your church board chair."

Andrew stilled, his thoughts racing. "How did you come up with that?"

"He's the only one who would know so much about the church, about the people, about Silas. I get this vibe from him I don't like. There's an innate sense of evil coming from him that he hides from most people." She paused, gathering her thoughts. "I had a phone, Andrew, that I used to send the name to Bill. But there's someone else, someone higher than him. Who, I'm not sure." She twisted, trying to break through the bonds. "We need out of here to help."

"I don't think we'll be able to. I don't think they'll let us loose other than when we need to be. They're too smart that way."

"And with you as a police officer, they're not going to take any chances."

"No, they're not. Let's hope Phoebe and Silas make it out okay and can get us help. Although I have no idea how they'd find us."

"I know. I don't think we were taken outside town. I was keeping track of the turns. They were driving in circles."

"Circles? Well, that makes sense, doesn't it? Confuse us so we don't know where we are."

They grew silent, lost in their thoughts. Andrew prayed that Phoebe had been found and was safe. He couldn't handle the thought of losing her. He listened closely, not hearing much of a sound from the rest of the building, but knowing someone was there. He twisted at his bonds, suddenly finding one loosening slightly. He paused, then went to work again on them. He had to get Madigan free and away.

Bill handed Silas a cup of coffee and then sat behind his desk, his hand running through his hair. Phoebe was with Lily.

"What happened, Silas? Walk me through it. I've heard from the others what happened up to when you were taken."

Silas sighed, bringing his thoughts back to the room he was in. He began to speak, praying that his memory would be accurate and he could relate to Bill exactly what went down.

Bill finally sat back. "Did you recognize anything about any of them?"

Silas shook his head. "I'm sorry. Not really. I was more concerned about Madigan and Phoebe and trying to see if they were with us and okay."

Bill nodded. "I get that. Now, about that name."

Silas shook his head, rising to pace. "I don't see that. How did they come up with that one?"

"Phoebe said Madigan was adamant it was someone in the church. She said your wife has picked up something from him and didn't quite know how to tell you, not without any evidence."

"I wish she had. Maybe we wouldn't be in the situation we are if she had." He turned to face Bill, his hands clenching against the chair back. "Where are they, Bill? Have they been taken out of town?"

"We don't know. I have people working on the name and searching records for properties belonging to him or his family. We'll find them, Silas." Bill stood as well, his eyes on his friend. "Now, what can I get you? Do you want me to call your Dad to come in?"

Silas shook his head. "If you do that, Mom comes and I don't want that. Call Matthew or Mitchell." He slumped back into the chair as Bill walked away, stopping for a moment to say a prayer for his pastor.

Lily found Bill in the break room, her eyes on the door she had walked through. "How's Silas?"

"Hurting. His faith has really been shaken. How's Phoebe?" He sipped from the cup of coffee he had just poured, grimacing at how strong it was.

"She's asleep, Bill. She stretched out on the couch in the locker room and fell asleep. She needs it."

Bill nodded. "Any word on properties yet?"

She shook her head. "He's buried them really deep. I have one of your friends searching titles for us."

"That's good. Listen. Watch Silas for me. I'm heading out for a bit. There's someone I need to talk to and I don't want to do it over the phone."

Lily watched as Bill walked away, then searched for Silas, finding him still in Bill's office, head bowed as he prayed as he had never prayed before.

$\mathcal{M}$adigan slumped in her chair, her bonds cutting into her wrists. She had tried to free herself, but it didn't work. She could hear Andrew moving around. She hated not being able to see and she certainly felt that God had abandoned them. She tensed as she felt a hand on her mouth, stifling her cry of surprise.

"Ssh, Madigan. It's me." Andrew's voice was soft in her ear. "I've managed to get free. Sit tight until I assess whether we can get out of here or not."

Andrew searched the room, finding a door to a back hallway. He inched it open, seeing no one. He returned, working on Madigan's bonds to release her. She pulled her blindfold from her face and blinked.

"Now what, Andrew?" Her voice was barely audible.

"I've found a way out. Come on." He led her from the room, down the hallway and stopped. He could hear voices from the other end of the house and prayed there was no one outside. He cracked open the back door and waited, finally stepping through and then leading Madigan to a shed near the back of the property.

"Wait here." He snuck around the building, not finding any vehicle they could escape in. He returned, finding Madigan watching the house intently. "What's going on?"

"They found out we're not there. We need to move, Andrew, and move quickly." She spun and began to run, Andrew following her.

They heard shouts behind them as their captors spied them and ran after them. Andrew finally grabbed Madigan's hand and pulled her into an empty building, searching for a hiding place for her. He shoved her into a crevice.

"Stay put. Don't come out unless it's me."

"Andrew! What about you?"

"I'll be fine." He turned as he heard the running footsteps and disappeared from her sight.

Madigan waited, not hearing anything. She finally made the decision she wasn't going to hide any more and stepped from the crevice, running towards the front of the building and the outdoors. She heard a shout behind her as she ran for the next building and turned her head. Sudden pain stopped her short and dropped her to the ground, her eyes closed.

Andrew struggled against the men who had re-captured him, a hand on his neck shoving his face into the grass, a knee grinding into his back, hands holding his arms out from his body. He was yanked to his feet and his hands bound once more. He searched for Madigan, drawing in a deep breath as he saw her lying still on the ground.

"Did you kill her?" The accusations were flying among the men.

"No. She turned just as I fired a warning shot. She did it to herself." The man who spoke knelt beside her. "She's still alive. Let's get them back to the house."

Andrew was shoved roughly into another room, the bonds disappearing from his wrists. Madigan's body was dumped on the floor. He rubbed at his wrists before he dropped to his knees, a shaking hand out to touch her. He hadn't meant for this to happen. Not at all.

He turned her head slightly to look at the wound and grimaced. It looked bad, bleeding heavily, and he had no way to stop it.

He rose, hurrying to the door, and hammering on it, calling that he needed water and cloths. That he needed to stop the bleeding unless they wanted her to die. He waited, his forehead resting on the door, gulping in air before pounding at the door again. He stepped back as he heard the key turn in the lock and the door pulled roughly open. Water and cloths were shoved at him as hard angry eyes stared at him. He stood, trying to get a sense of who it was. He felt that he knew the man, just couldn't place him. He winced as the door slammed shut, the loudness of it echoing through the room.

He dropped to his knees beside Madigan, soaking a cloth and wiping away the blood. He winced at the gash cutting through her hair. He tried as best he could to wrap cloths around her head, putting pressure on the wound. He sat back on his heels, knowing he had done the best he could, but with no guarantees it would work.

Lord, she's hurt. I need to keep her alive and get her back to Silas. I don't know how he'd survive without her. Lead my people to us. I have no idea why we're where we are but You do.

He checked the bandage and saw the blood flow had lessened. He raised her head enough to get her to swallow some water. He was out of his element here, he knew.

He sat back against the wall, his thoughts going to the men who had re-captured them, frowning as he concentrated on them. Then, he groaned. He knew who the man was now. And Madigan was right. He was from the church, just not the one she had named.

Three hours later, the door opened and Andrew was pulled out of the room and shoved into a chair, a light blinding him. He felt the newspaper he was forced to hold, and frowned. He could vaguely see camera flashes and his heart sank. They were going to the next step, and his policy was that they didn't go along with the demands of kidnappers, knowing it very seldom worked out.

Bill shook Silas awake. "Silas, we have news."

Silas sat up, rubbing at his eyes, then running his hand down his face, the stubble rough against his hands. "What news?"

"We received a package, with a picture of Andrew holding today's newspaper. They're not making any demands as yet, which is odd."

"That is strange. Has Art or Ray been around?"

Bill nodded. "They both called. I just told them they couldn't talk to any one of you, that we were still getting your statements. I don't want you to talk to them at all. Your Dad is stepping in on Sundays for you until you can. The board asked if he would."

Silas nodded. "Thanks, Bill. That takes some of the pressure off." He sat back, despondency in his very bearing. "I'm not sure I'll continue as pastor here."

"Don't let this get you down to that point, Silas. Your work here isn't finished, not by a long shot. Our staff is fielding calls from your people, giving tips, offering encouragement and prayers, offering whatever support they can."

Silas nodded. A frown appeared. "Who else do you suspect?"

Bill shook his head. "I can't tell you that, you know that, Silas. I can't compromise the investigation." He picked up the photo he had taken of the package. "This is strange. Why would they send this other than to let us know Andrew is still alive?"

"Nothing on Madi?" Silas looked up in hope.

"Nothing about her. She'll likely be the next photo we get."

Silas sat in silence. "What can we do to put pressure on them, Bill? To find out what they actually want?"

Bill shook his head. "We're working on a plan, Silas, but we still need a crucial bit of information." He looked around as Lily appeared, a folder in her hand.

"Take a lot at this, Bill. Somehow, Emma knew we needed help."

Bill opened the folder, a breath of relief passing through him. "Have you researched this?"

Lily shook her head. "That's where I'm heading now. I just wanted you to have this copy. I guess Leah's aunt talked to Emma and let her know what was happening."

"Bless Mrs. Bradshaw." Silas looked up, a small ray of hope awakening in his heart. "Will what Emma gave you help?"

Bill nodded. "It should. Pray that it does." He looked around, seeing Don standing in the hallway. "Silas, I'm sending you and Phoebe off with Don and his team. We'll keep in close touch, but I need both of you somewhere safe."

Silas sighed, even as he nodded, knowing that this step was necessary. "Find my Madi, Bill. Find Phoebe's Andrew. Bring them home."

❀ ❀ ❀ ❀

Madigan rolled to her side, the pain in her head almost unbearable. She groaned and felt hands on her.

"Silas? Is that you? Where am I?"

"It's Andrew, Madigan. How are you feeling?"

"Horrible. I think I'm going to be sick."

Andrew swept her up and carried her to the small bathroom he had discovered just off the room. The sink was stained and badly chipped and the toilet wasn't much better, but it would do. He set her on the floor and stepped back, assessing her for a moment, before pulling the door closed and walking across to the one window they had. It was too small for either of them to get out of. He had rubbed away at the dirt until he could see out, but it didn't help much. He had no idea where they were.

He turned as he heard the door open and Madigan appeared, holding onto the door frame, her other hand on her head.

"Andrew, is it night? How long have we been here?" She squinted as she tried to see.

Andrew walked back towards her, not quite sure what to say. "It's afternoon, Madigan. Are you having trouble seeing?"

She nodded as she held out a hand in front of her. "I can't see anything, Andrew." Panic was setting in. "It's all black."

He helped her back down to the floor and rechecked her bandage. "You were shot at and hit in the head. I've tried to stop the bleeding, but you really need medical care." He turned to look at the door, knowing that wasn't about to happen. "Here, have some water. We need to keep fluids down you."

She swallowed, then laid back down, her head pillowed on her arm. "Wake me when Silas gets back, okay?"

Andrew stared at her as she drifted back to sleep, his mouth in a thin grim line.

Now what, Lord? She can't see. I can't get her to help. Please, Lord, work in this. Get us out of here.

Andrew looked up as the door opened and two men entered, heading for Madigan.

"Leave her alone."

They spun to Andrew, ready to fight him, but stopped at his next words.

"She can't help you. She can't see anything." He looked back up, his eyes searching them. "Are you satisfied now?"

The two men shared a look and then left, needing to speak with their leader. He would be extremely unhappy, knowing that he couldn't use Madigan as leverage.

Andrew dropped his chin to his chest, his thoughts dark, then lifting his heart in prayer. God was the only one who'd be able to get them out of this, he knew.

Silas stood at the kitchen counter in the safe house, staring out the window, his thoughts on Madigan. Where is she, Lord? Is she okay? Have they hurt her? Please, dear Lord, bring her back to me. He turned as he heard footsteps and watched as Don stopped in the doorway.

"Silas, what can I do for you?"

Silas shrugged. "I have no idea, Don. What do you suggest?"

Don pointed at a chair, sliding into one himself. "I know who you suspect. I would say you're right. But have you looked at any of his family or friends as well?"

Silas shook his head. "Bill's supposed to be doing that. Why would I?"

"Because you may be the key we need to get Madigan and Andrew back and sooner than later. So, who all is in that family?"

Silas sat back, finally rising to find a pad of paper and a pen. He sat down again, his thoughts concentrating on names. He eventually slid the paper across the table to Don.

Don read through them, nodding. "Some of these I knew but not all of them. I'm going to have my team work on this. Hang in there, Silas. We'll get them back."

Silas nodded, suddenly exhausted to the point he couldn't see. He stumbled to his feet and down to the room they had assigned him, not seeing the concern on Phoebe's face as she stood in the living doorway. She sighed, heading for the kitchen, hoping there was something in the cupboards she could make or cook or something like that.

Bill stood watching her, noting the sadness she was trying so hard to hide.

"Phoebe?"

She spun at his voice, not having her him come in. "Bill! Any word?"

He shook his head. "Nothing yet. We're working around the clock on this one, Phoebe. We'll find him."

She nodded. "I know you will, but in what condition? Alive or dead?"

Bill sighed, knowing she was correct. "We're doing everything we can, Phoebe. We going back through everything, talking to family members, trying to find properties he owns."

She nodded. "I know, but it doesn't make it any easier."

"No, it doesn't.   What are you concocting?"

She looked down at the counter, realizing she hadn't solved anything with her work, instead making a huge mess she now had to clean up. "I have no idea. A mess by the looks of it." She raised her head, her eyes focused on the wall, a frown on her face. "Bill, is there an old house near the edge of town, not in too bad of shape, Victorian in design, with overgrown hedges and vegetation?"

Bill's hand stilled as he was reaching for the coffee pot and he stared at her. "There is. The old Waters place. Why?"

"Try that place. Please!" She turned tortured eyes to him. "They're there. I just know it. Please, will you, for me?"

He watched her, knowing she was speaking from her heart. "How do you know it?"

She shrugged. "God just showed me. And you need to hurry. Madigan's in trouble."

Bill spun, his voice calling for Don. A few quick words and Bill was out the door, Don on his heels. They quickly headed for the Waters house, not calling in reinforcements until they were sure.

They stood, hidden in the growth of the hedge, searching the outside area. Don touched Bill's arm and pointed. Bill nodded and pointed off the one side, three fingers in the air. Don took off quietly for the opposite of the yard as Bill crouched down and crept towards the man walking around the house, coming up behind him unawares. A few quick movements and the man was down, gagged and handcuffed, searched for weapons that Bill tucked into his coat. Don helped roll the man into the hedge and pull branches back over the opening.

The two men crept up the steps to the back door, listening for anyone who was in the house. Bill squeezed the knob and carefully turned it, not hearing the expected squeak or creak of the door. He slipped inside, Don at his heels, and waited, listening once more. Finger in the air, he pointed in front of him and Don nodded.

They searched the rooms as they came to them, finding nothing until they came to a locked door. Bill touched the key, not sure what he would find on the other side. He unlocked the door and opened it, weapon held at the ready, quickly pointing it up in the air as he saw Andrew standing there, fists clenched, a look of surprise on his face as he saw the two. Andrew pointed at Madigan and rushed to sweep her up, quickly following Bill and Don from the house and to their vehicle, not saying anything. Don stopped and pulled their prisoner from the hedge, shoving him roughly into the back seat of the car.

"Where first, Andrew?" Don turned to watch Madigan, concern colouring his face at how she looked.

"The hospital, Bill. Madigan needs care. She was hit by a bullet yesterday. I tried to stop the bleeding, but she's been vomiting and says she can't see anything."

Bill and Don shared a look before Bill asked. "What about you, Andrew?"

Andrew shrugged, as he watched the hospital getting closer. "I'm fine. Bumps and bruises and scrapes, but nothing like Madigan." He stared at his friends. "Phoebe? Is she…?" His voice died away.

"She's fine, Andrew, both she and Silas. Don has them tucked away somewhere safe. I'll drop you and Madigan off here with Don and send some officers over as well. We'll keep it as low key as we can."

"One thing, Bill. One of our captors is Ray's son, Bobbie."

Bill nodded. "We figured as much. They're a nasty bunch, it seems. How'd your friend there get involved with them?"

The prisoner glared at them, refusing to speak.

Andrew shook his head as he stared down at Madigan, worried about his friend. "There are six lackies, plus the leader. But I think you'll find someone over him. Try Ray Walker, Art, Ray's son, Bobbie, his nephew Joe, his daughter, Megan, and three of their friends."

The captive stared at him, wondering how he had it figured out. Andrew caught the look and shook his head.

"Did you really think you could hide that well? We know you people too well. You give yourselves away."

Bill pulled the door open and Andrew gathered Madigan into his arms, heading for the back entrance to the Emergency Department, Don keeping step with him. Bill headed for the detachment, intent on booking their suspect and attempting to interview him.

There were exclamations of surprise as Andrew and Don walked in before Andrew was pointed to one of the examination rooms at the back. He laid Madigan down and stepped back, watching as the nurses and finally John rushed to work on her.

John stepped back, assessing Andrew, pointing to the room across the hall. Andrew turned, stumbling with fatigue, almost going down until Don rammed a shoulder under his arm and wrapped his other arm around him, helping him to the bed there. Andrew swung his feet up, fatigue washing over him.

"Andrew? What happened?"

He pried his eyes open. John stood beside him, hand on his wrist, watching him closely. "Madigan was shot yesterday. It creased her. I tried to help. Tried to stop the bleeding. I couldn't get her out, get her to help." He paused to control his emotions. "She's been vomiting. And she says she can't see, everything's black is how she put it." Andrew's eyes slid shut and he slept, knowing that they were safe.

John and Don exchanged a glance, not quite knowing what to say.

"I'll stay with him, John. Go see to Madigan. I'll get Silas and Phoebe here shortly."

John nodded, his footsteps hurried on the tiled floor as he walked back to Madigan. Quiet words were exchanged. He pulled back the cloths Andrew had used and he frowned, a tight look on his face, and he called for imaging to be done stat.

He turned and looked across the hall at Andrew, seeing Don standing just outside his door, where he could watch both rooms.

"John? We need to kept quiet that they're here. We can't risk their lives." Don's soft words drifted to John, who nodded.

"I get you. Are your people on the way in?"

Don nodded down the hall. "Two are here now. I'll like one to go with Madigan wherever you take her."

❀ ❀ ❀ ❀

Bill slipped quietly into the house, speaking with the new team members Don had brought on board, Sally and Tony.

"We have them, guys. Madigan's hurt. We need to get these two to them." He headed down the hall to find Silas as Sally went searching for Phoebe.

"Phoebe?" Sally's voice cut into Phoebe's thoughts and she turned from the window she was looking out.

"Sally? You have news?"

Sally smiled. "We do. Andrew's at the hospital. Bill says he's fine. Come on. Let's get you to your guy."

Phoebe paused, saying a quick prayer before she reached for a jacket and followed Sally.

Bill stood for a moment, watching as Silas slept, seeing the stress and devastation on his face, before he reached to shake him away.

"Silas. Wake up! We need to get you over to the hospital." He stepped back as Silas roused and swung his legs over the edge of the bed and sat.

"What was that you said, Bill?" He looked up, rubbing at his eyes.

"We have Madigan, Silas. She's hurt and in the hospital. But we have them both."

Silas stared at him for a moment, then surged to his feet, his hand grasping his jacket and then the front door knob. A hand on his arm stopped him.

"Let me go first, Silas." Bill waited until Silas stepped back. "We'll get you there but we need to do that in one piece."

Footsteps that were almost running sounded in the hospital hallway before they slid to an abrupt halt at Madigan's doorway. Silas stood there, hand on the doorframe to catch himself, before he walked softly over to the bed, his eyes on no one but his wife.

John stepped back, his eyes assessing Silas, then flickering over to Madigan, waiting to see if she would rouse with Silas there. They had not been able to wake her.

Silas' hands trembled as he reached for his wife. "Madi, sweetheart, it's me. Wake up." He touched her face gently, his hand stopping at the bandage before he looked up. "John?"

John walked forward, resting his hands on the bed end. "There's no fracture, no bleeding in the brain. A severe concussion I would suspect."

"What aren't you telling me?"

John sighed, knowing he had to be completely honest. "Andrew mentioned that she couldn't see, that everything seemed dark."

"Her vision? Will it come back?"

"It should. There is no physical reason for her not to see. I think she's shutting down something that she doesn't want to admit."

Silas nodded, his eyes back on Madigan. "What now, John?"

"We're moving her to a secluded area of the medical wing. Don's people will be watching her and Bill has assigned officers as well. She'll be protected. We'll limit who gets into her."

Silas nodded. "No one from the church. Just myself and whatever medical team you need with her. Her parents and brother only for short visits. I have to keep her safe now that she's back."

"I hear you." John looked up as he heard voices in the hallway and left.

Silas searched and found a chair, setting it beside the bed, reaching for Madigan's hand, studying her beloved face. Lord, bring her back. Heal her. Restore her sight.

She moved slightly, grimacing with the pain, before she reached blindly to raise herself.

"Madi?"

"I'm going to be sick. I need a basin or the bathroom."

Silas' arm supported her even as he held the basin, reaching for a warm washcloth the nurse handed him to wash her face when she was done. She laid her head on his shoulder and shuddered.

"Madi. You're safe. You're with me." His voice was low enough that she barely heard him.

"Silas? You're okay?" She tilted her head back and squinted, vaguely seeing his face. "What did you do? You're blurry."

He grinned down at her, before he sobered and frowned. She could see his face?

"You can see me?"

She nodded, then winced. "Why'd you have me do that? It hurts." She closed her eyes, her hand clenching his. "I can see you, not totally clear yet. Why? Was I having trouble seeing?"

"Andrew said you were. But John says your vision will come back." He looked up as Bill stopped by the bed. "Bill's here, sweetheart. Care to talk to him?"

"No. Tell him to go away."

Bill laughed softly. "Just a couple of questions, Madigan, and then I'll go away. Glad we found you. Did you recognize anyone?" Bill had asked the nurse to step out of the room and close the door before he spoke.

She nodded, sadness sweeping across her face. "I did. Ray was there and his son and daughter, I think. I heard other voices but I wasn't in any shape to recognize them." She sat up, hand going to her head as it pounded. "Andrew? Tell me he's okay."

"He is, Madigan. He's across the hall with Phoebe."

"Oh, thank God. I thought we'd die there, you know." She slipped back into sleep, not realizing she was still talking, saying that God didn't care, that she was broken, and that Silas wouldn't want her any more.

Silas' heart sank at the words. What had they done to her? He shared a look with Bill, who shook his head.

"She'll be fine, Silas. A lot of captives will go through something similar. It's not unusual, given what you two have been through."

Silas nodded. "Thanks again, Bill. Where's the investigation standing now?"

"We're getting there. Some of the people have disappeared and we're tracking their flight. Art is one I'm concerned about.

He may try and get to you two or to Andrew and Phoebe.”

“What about Andrew? How is he?”

“Dehydrated, exhausted. Bumps and bruises and scrapes. He said they had gotten away at one point and then they were recaptured. Madigan was running and turned wrong. That’s how she was shot.”

Silas nodded. “Thanks for letting me know, Bill.” He turned to face the door, torn between being a husband and being a pastor.

“Silas?” He looked up at Bill’s quiet voice. “Go. See Andrew. I’ll stay with your wife until you come back.”

Silas stared down at Madigan before he dropped a kiss on her cheek and then turned to walk across the hall. Phoebe looked up at him, tears sparkling on her face.

“He’s sleeping, Silas. I don’t think he’s slept the whole time he was gone.”

“He needs it. I won’t waken him. Let me pray with you two, though.”

Phoebe watched as he hesitated before leaving. “How’s Mads?”

He looked up, a small smile on his face. “She’s in a lot of pain but her vision is coming back. John said they'll be moving them upstairs soon."

"I'm so glad she's recovering, Silas. God has been good."

Silas nodded. "He has been. But Madigan, I don't know. She say something about God not caring and being broken as she went back to sleep."

Phoebe drew in a deep breath. "It happened to me, Silas. I felt the same way just before Andrew rescued me. You know how hard it was for me. We've talked about things not even Andrew has heard about but that I still have to tell him. Mads will get there. Treat her as the treasure you always have."

"And she is a treasure, now isn't she? Thanks, Phoebe. I'm glad you and Madi are friends."

"So am I, Silas. I know how much Andrew treasures your friendship. It would be tough if we weren't friends. I like your wife. She's got a refreshing way of looking at life and talking to God."

Silas nodded, even as he smiled. "She does at that, doesn't she?" He turned. "Let me know if I can do anything for you two."

Phoebe nodded even as he walked from the room, a sound from Andrew drawing her attention back to him. She reached for his hand and felt his grip on hers tighten even as his eyes opened and he looked around.

"Phoebe?"

"You're safe, Andrew. Bill and Don found you and got you out."

"Madigan?" Andrew tried to sit up, finally giving up as his head spun. He stared at the IV line running to his hand.

"She's improving, love. Silas says her vision is coming back."

"I'm glad. She frightened me when she asked if it was night and that she couldn't see." He reached up to touch her face. "And you're fine?"

She nodded. "We are. I just don't get it though, love. Why did they separate us like that?"

"To make sure we cooperated with them. They were planning on using us against each other, I suspect. Now, how long am I in here for?"

She laughed as she leaned over the bed, her head on his chest. "For as long as you need to be, love. I'm not leaving either."

Chapter 21

*M*adigan turned restlessly in her sleep, her hands going up to protect her head even as Silas reached for her hands, to clasp them tight. He knew it wasn't over for them yet, not by a long shot. He sighed, his eyes raising up as he prayed for his wife, for his friends, for his church, for himself.

"Silas?"

He looked down to find Madigan's eyes open and on him. "What is it, sweetheart?"

"Where am I?" She tried to sit up and he sat on the edge of the bed, his arms around her, cradling her against him.

"You're in the hospital. You've been here for two days now."

"I'm safe?"

"You are. How's your head?"

"The headache is much better. And I don't feel sick any more. What happened? Everything about that time seems black."

"It was. You lost your sight for a few days after you were shot." He cradled her back against him from where she had leaned back to look at him, shock in her face at what he said. "Andrew looked after you. It wasn't even a day later Bill and Don found you both."

"Remind me to thank them, will you?" She sighed, content to be where she was. "How'd you two get away? Andrew was so worried about Phoebe."

"It really doesn't matter, does it? We were found and released. Actually, they forgot to look the door when they took you two away and we just walked out and found Bill. Now we're together. We need to get you better."

She nodded, wincing at the slight pain coursing through her head. "Has Bill been around? I need to talk to him."

"He has been, but you have already. You've given him the names he needed of who kidnapped you."

"I have? I don't remember."

"No, I didn't think you had. Now that you're awake, they'll release you home." He watched her face, seeing the conflicting emotions crossing it. "What is it, sweetheart?"

"This broke me, Silas. It took me right down to nothing. I didn't even think God cared any more."

Tears gathered in Silas' eyes at her confession and he dropped a kiss on the top of her head, even as he prayed for healing for her.

❀ ❀ ❀ ❀

Two weeks later, Silas settled Madigan into what had become her pew in church, the second one from the front on the right side, right beside the piano before heading for the platform and the start of the service. Silas looked over his people, content once more, just still apprehensive as Art had not yet been found. Andrew and Bill were still searching but he had hidden himself well. All the others had been found and were facing long prison terms once their trials concluded but that was still down the road. No matter how much they were questioned, they couldn't or wouldn't say where Art hidden himself.

As he approached the pulpit for the pastoral prayer, he stopped, horror coursing through him. Madigan had not yet sat back down but couldn't. The eyes of the congregation were glued to her. His heart sank. Art had found her.

Madigan tried to communicate desperately with Silas with her eyes. Art had his arm around her in a tight bond, a knife held to her throat. She didn't dare move. She could hear rustling behind her but couldn't look.

Silas stopped, his eyes on Art. "What do you want, Art?"

"My son and daughter out of jail. Arrange that and I'll let your woman go."

Silas shook his head in a sorrowful manner, his eyes on Madigan. "You know that I can't do that, Art. I don't have that power."

"You do if you want her to live. Get Andrew in here. Get him to arrange it."

Andrew stopped a couple of pews back from Madigan, his eyes on Art, waiting for an opportunity to make a move. They had been looking all over for him but he had not expected him to show up in church in this manner. Bill moved quietly up the outside aisle, watching for an opportunity to take Art down.

Words went back and forth between Silas and Art, Silas attempting to talk Art into surrendering, Art demanding his family's release. Neither of them budged.

Madigan was growing desperate. She knew Silas would attempt something soon, and it wouldn't be pretty, whatever it was. She sighed, her body slumping somewhat, throwing Art's aim with the knife away from her throat. She stepped down hard on his foot and then flung her head backwards into his face. Art howled with pain as his grip on her relaxed and she dove from him to the floor, crawling away from him under the pew towards the piano.

Andrew and Bill were there in seconds, Art handcuffed and the knife on the floor. Andrew showed Art towards Bill, nodding towards the door as he reached with a gloved hand to pick up the knife. Silas was off the platform, seated on the floor, Madigan in his arms as she sobbed. The congregation sat in stunned silence before voices broke out. Andrew sighed. The witness list was large. He reached for his phone, calling in additional officers. He wouldn't be leaving any time soon.

He stepped around the pew and dropped into a crouch near Silas, his eyes on Madigan.

"Madigan?" His voice was quiet.

Madigan refused to look up, her face buried against Silas, her arms tight around him. Silas shook his head at Andrew.

"Madigan, can you look up, please?" Silas reached to touch her face and she jerked back. "Madi? Were you hurt?"

She shook her head. "I don't think so. He's scared me." She looked at Andrew. "He's the one, Andrew, the one who told Jerry to lock me up, and then he's the one who let me go. Why?"

Andrew reached to touch her shoulder. "We'll find out, Madigan. Silas, take her to your office. I'll have Sam stand guard for you."

Silas rose, then swept Madigan into his arms, heading out of the sanctuary, not hearing the hush that came over the people, or hearing the new board chair step up to the front and start praying for them all. His only concern was his wife.

Chapter 22

Madigan turned as she felt Silas' arm come around her as she stood on their back deck and she leaned into his strength. It had been two weeks since the incident in the church and she was just starting to finally feel safe.

Andrew studied them for a moment before he approached them, Phoebe at his side. The younger couple had given a dinner for all their friends and families, who now mingled both inside and outside the house, enjoying the crispness of an early autumn evening.

"How are you two doing now?" Andrew's keen eyes assessed them.

Madigan shrugged. "Getting there, Andrew. I've had a lot to deal with, all those repressed memories.   Maybe if I had remembered before, none of this would have happened."

"I think it would have to someone, if not you, then someone else." Andrew shared a look with Silas. "He had gone about as far as he could go and not get caught."

"So, why did he do what he did? Why'd he drag so many people into it all?"

"He needed a locksmith to be able to get his gang into homes and businesses. That where Ray came in. He found out something on Ray and used it to blackmail him. Art's a nasty piece of work who fooled almost everyone. He also blackmailed the lawyer, judge, etc., whoever it was that was involved with Jerry Lake. Everyone but you, Madigan. You knew, even if you couldn't remember."

She shuddered. "He has such a sense of evil about him. I'm surprised more people couldn't feel it." She looked up at Silas. "I think you did, love, but you weren't sure what you were picking up on."

Silas agreed. "I know. There was always something about him I just wasn't sure of. Ray was the same way. He must be carrying a load of guilt."

"He is, Silas. He has asked if you would come see him. He doesn't think Madigan would, even though he would like to apologize for his part in what happened."

Madigan and Silas shared a look. "Let us pray on that one, Andrew. It may take a bit, but at some point we will." Silas' words had Madigan nodding.

"So what drove Art then?" Madigan turned back to look at Andrew.

"He had been in love with your mother, Madigan, years ago in high school. She never liked or trusted him. She won't say why but other women have talked to me. He's a nasty piece of work. He blames her for everything he's done, not taking responsible for his own actions. He had Jerry lock you up and had planned to demand a ransom for you, but when you panicked in the dark and shut down, he felt he had had enough revenge. He didn't realize that it would affect you for so long or so badly. He had no regrets over that. He dragged his son and daughter and nephew and their friends in with promises of easy money and drugs."

"Drugs?" Silas was puzzled over that one.

"Drugs. He was one of the drug suppliers we had been looking for. It all comes down to greed and blackmail. He's been the one behind every single thing that happened to you two. He kidnapped me to try and hinder the investigation and if that didn't work, then he planned to use me to find out what was happening. He's responsible for Jerry Lake's death as well. As to why, he's not saying. He was after you, Silas, just because he thought you had found out, somehow, what he was up to."

Madigan stared out across the yard, not seeing Silas, Phoebe and Andrew watching her.

"I feel sorry for him. He could have had so much but threw it all away. He's a pitiful creature really, but God does still love him, doesn't He? Maybe while he is prison he'll find that out."

Silas stared at his wife before he tightened his hold on her and dropped a kiss to her cheek. "Such wisdom, sweetheart. You're right. God is the only one who can reach him now. I doubt he'll ever speak with us."

Finally alone, the evening sparkling with star diamonds against a black velvet sky, Silas drew his wife down into the swing, his foot setting it in motion. Madigan snuggled close in his arms, content, finally free of the ghosts of her past. They sat that way for a long while before Silas spoke.

"Your mom asked if we wanted to redo our vows with all the trimmings. I had told her when we first married we might and she could make some plans.”

Madigan turned her head to look up at him. “Did you?” She thought for a moment before she shook her head. “I don’t think so. It won’t change the fact that we married. It’s an expense I’d rather not do.”

Silas nodded, having come to the same conclusion. Before he could speak, she continued.

“Why don’t we just have an open house after church one Sunday, for our families and our people? No gifts unless it’s to a charity.”

Silas hugged her close. “I like that idea.” He tilted his head so he could see her. “Have I told you lately how much I love you?”

She smiled. “You have, but I’ll never tire of hearing it. I love you too.” Her smile disappeared as he claimed her lips in a long kiss before sitting back.

“Thank you, sweetheart, for being just who you are. God knew we needed one another.”

They watched as the full moon rose, talk between them sweet and low. They finally rose, heading for the house. Silas stood for a moment, his face raised to the heavens, a thankful prayer raised as well as a prayer for wisdom he'd need over the years.

Dear Readers:

Thank you for choosing to read *Strong Courage*, the story of Pastor Silas Peters and Madigan Browne. Silas became very vocal at some point in the His Warriors series that he wanted to have his story told. I needed a strong woman to go with his courage and strength and Madigan became that person.

As broken as she felt, she still knew she was loved deeply by her family and eventually by her husband. With his love, she was able to find the courage she needed to face the past.

What do you need to face this day, where you have no strength or courage of your own? We have God's strength in our lives. We are not alone, no matter how dark it seems.

Joshua 1:9 has been a favourite verse of mine since I memorized back as a teenager through the Bible Memorization Association where you memorized a certain number of verses for about 10 to 15 weeks. I have gone back to it so many times.

God never fails, never quits, never ever leaves us, no matter how black it is. Trust Him for that.

God bless each one of you.

Ronna